Peanut Jones

and the
Twelve Portals

Jones

Written and illustrated by

ROB BIDDULPH

MACMILLAN CHILDREN'S BOOKS

First published 2022 by
Macmillan Children's Books
an imprint of Pan Macmillan
The Smithson, 6 Briset Street, London EC1M 5NR
EU representative:
Macmillan Publishers Ireland Ltd, 1st Floor,
The Liffey Trust Centre, 117–126 Sheriff Street
Upper Dublin 1, D01 YC43
Associated companies throughout the world
www.panmacmillan.com

ISBN 978-1-5290-4056-2

3 5 7 9 8 6 4 2

A CIP catalogue record for this book is
available from the British Library.

Printed and Bound in Great Britain by
Bell & Bain Ltd. Glasgow

MIX
Paper | Supporting
responsible forestry
FSC® C116313

For Petra,
who brings the sunshine

Prologue

To their great surprise, the door opened. Four pairs of eyes peered into the cool, dark room.

Silence.

Feeling brave, the older girl pushed against the wafer-thin surface. It crackled as it swung further on its papery hinges. Tentatively, the children crept through.

The scent of turpentine mixed with cheap soap hit their nostrils as they jumped down and stood on the dusty floor. Two red lights, a couple of metres from the ground, were glowing at the back of the room. The younger boy with the big hair gulped.

'Who's there?' he said. 'I-I can hear breathing.'

Something small with claws scuttled across the floor in front of them.

., that's
had enough.'
urned to leave, but
girl grabbed his jacket and
led him back.

'Hello?' she said into the darkness, her voice full of hope. 'Is anybody in here with us?'

This time, nothing.

Suddenly, dazzling light flooded their vision and all four of them instinctively brought their hands up to their faces. After a few seconds, they stopped rubbing their eyes and lowered their arms.

As her sight adjusted, the girl watched the tall figure in front of them turn away, put the torch down, and reach up to his right. He slid open a metal grate and four diagonal brushstrokes of light raced into the room, painting one side of him in bright, iridescent colours. Long, unruly hair, shimmering with warm reds, deep oranges and rich golds, tumbled down over his shoulders. As he slowly turned to face his visitors, he revealed a long beard.

The girl stepped forward and rubbed her eyes again. Could it be? Underneath all that hair? Was it him?

'Hello, Peanut,' said the man.

She exhaled. And then she smiled.

'Hello, Dad.'

Part One
...in which Peanut's
eyes are opened

1

Earlier That Day

Peanut Jones picked up the last of the marker pens and carefully slid it into the custom-made slot on her new artistic utility belt. It was a perfect fit, just as the paintbrushes, the charcoal block, the brush pen, the ink roller, the pots of black-and-white ink, the stamps, the can of spray paint and the small tin of watercolours had been. The belt was fully loaded and ready to go. Well, *almost* fully loaded. One slot remained empty.

This was the second iteration of her bandolier. The first version had been taken from her a few months ago when she and her friends had been imprisoned in the Spire, a huge tower at the centre of Chroma, the Illustrated City. But far worse than losing the bandolier had been the loss of her all-important magic pencil. It had been stolen by a small man wearing a white fedora, after an incident involving a remote detonator (given to Peanut, her friend Rockwell and her sister Little-Bit by a talking alligator) and several thousand exploding mechanical fish.

Peanut reached over to her desk and picked up the wooden box that was sitting on top of her exercise books. It was full to the brim with small, yellow Post-it notes. Each one had been decorated with a picture drawn by her dad – he used to hide one inside her school lunchbox every day to cheer her up as she ate her sandwiches. But that was before he suddenly went missing. She ran her fingers across the two words carved into the lid: 'Little Tail'. It was inside the secret compartment at the bottom of this box that she had first found Conté's Pencil Number One, the magic pencil, and soon after its discovery she'd realised that whatever it drew became real. That, in turn, had started a chain of events that led to her drawing a door, opening it, and stepping through into Chroma, the Illustrated City.

The driving beat of the drums, guitars and keyboards coming from her radio faded as the DJ's voice kicked back in.

'The Beatles there with "Get Back" – one of their very best! And now at five o'clock, it's time for the top-of-the-hour news headlines, read to you today by Benedict Hughes.'

Peanut opened the lid and picked up one of the Post-it notes. On it, Dad had drawn a perfect miniature version of *The Great Wave off Kanagawa* by Hokusai. *How appropriate*, she thought. At various points over the past year she'd felt as if she were in the eye of a similarly overwhelming storm. Just recently, however, it seemed as though the clouds had parted slightly, and one or two beams of sunlight were beginning to break through. Finally, there was a glimmer of hope.

'One of the world's most famous paintings, Guernica *by Pablo Picasso, today became the tenth priceless work of art to mysteriously disintegrate in the last three months.'*

Peanut's eyes flicked from the Hokusai Post-it note to the radio.

'The bizarre turn of events happened just before Madrid's Museo Reina Sofia opened this morning. Renowned art historian Diana Drown described it as a tragedy to end all tragedies. "What was once the most moving and powerful anti-war painting in history is now just a medium-sized pile of silvery grey powder on the gallery floor. I haven't stopped crying all day."'

Peanut's coppery topknot swayed from side to side as she shook her head. *Another one?* She thought to herself. *This has definitely got Mr White's fingerprints all over it. The sooner we get back to Chroma the better.*

Mr White. The man who had stolen the pencil from her in Chroma. The man who had imprisoned her in the Spire. The man who wanted to rid the world of all its creativity.

'In other news, a woman in Buckinghamshire today found a turnip in her local supermarket that looks exactly like the Prime Minister. Barbara Armitage, from Chalfont St Peter, described the likeness as uncanny. "And, what's more, it would probably make a better job of running the country!"...'

Peanut stuck the Hokusai drawing to the wall, switched off the radio and turned to face her newest collection of Post-it notes which were stuck to the wardrobe door.

These notes had started to show up in her lunchbox on a daily basis a couple of weeks after she had returned from Chroma. Most of them featured abstract shapes made up of one or two thick, black lines, but some were almost blank. Almost. On every one, the words 'Love you forever x' were written in tiny, cursive handwriting. Her dad's tiny, cursive

handwriting to be exact. He had written the same thing on every single packed-lunch Post-it note he had ever drawn for her.

When Dad had disappeared, Peanut's lunchtime notes had also stopped. So she had been delighted when, three months ago, she'd found one nestled between her sandwich and her cereal bar. Since then, a new note had appeared every day – in fact, on some days there had been more than one.

This was her glimmer of hope. Not only was it proof that Dad was alive, but also that he was trying to tell her something. She just needed to work out what that something was.

2
The Sleepover

he bedroom door swung open and a small girl with a big voice came rushing in.

'PEEEEEEEAAAAANUUUUUUTTTT!'

Little-Bit Jones jumped up on to the bed and immediately started rummaging through the Post-it notes in the box.

'Which one's your favourite?' she said, spreading a selection out on the duvet. 'I like Daffy Duck.

I've always thought him vastly underrated in the Looney Tunes canon. His insatiable ego and explosive temperament are perfect comedy fodder, and 1953's *Duck Amuck* is a classic of the genre.'

Peanut stared, wide-eyed, at her five-year-old sister. Her precocious intelligence never failed to surprise. It had also proved to be incredibly useful during their adventures together in Chroma.

'Anyway, can we go soon? I'm bored. If we waste any more time, another painting might turn to dust.' Little-Bit was already feeling the drag of summer holiday listlessness, despite only starting school the previous year. 'Also, I can't wait to see Doodle again! Marley's new puppy is cute and everything, but I think a magic dog like Doodle is even better!'

'GIRLS! IT'S GONE FIVE O'CLOCK!'

Tracey Jones, their mother, was standing at the bottom of the stairs with her hair wrapped up in a towel. She was halfway through painting her fingernails the same colour as the dark red jumpsuit she was wearing.

'YOU NEED TO LEAVE NOW IF YOU'RE GOING TO GET TO THE SCIENCE MUSEUM IN TIME!' she called.

Little-Bit tried to stifle a giggle.

'She thinks we're actually going to go to the Science Museum, doesn't she?' she whispered through her fingers. 'As if!'

'I do feel bad about lying,' said Peanut, 'but we can't run the risk of her telling *him* where we're really headed.'

She picked up the bandolier, folded it twice and carefully put it into her sports bag.

'Ah. There you are!' said Mum, looking up from her nails as the sisters appeared on the landing. 'Now, have you got everything you need? Oh, I'm so excited for you! They didn't have museum sleepovers when I was a girl. How I would have loved to spend the night among all that lovely scientific, er . . . stuff. Peanut, I'm so glad you're finally embracing the important things in life.'

Peanut sighed as she walked down the stairs. Her relationship with her mother had been strained since Dad had vanished. Mum had

been worried at first, but after he'd sent a mysterious postcard from Mexico City telling them all to forget him, she'd become angry, thinking he had abandoned them because of his failings as an artist. But Peanut had never believed that story. In fact, it seemed to Peanut that these days Mum blamed everything that ever went wrong on art and creativity in general. Only last year she had insisted that Peanut leave her beloved Melody High and attend St Hubert's School for the Seriously Scientific and Terminally Mathematic. If Peanut's heart hadn't already been broken because of Dad's disappearance, that had certainly done the trick.

Mum licked her finger and rubbed her eldest daughter's forehead vigorously until she was satisfied it was clean.

'Right then, off you go. Have fun.' She kissed them both on the cheek. 'I'm sorry I can't give you a lift to the station, but Milton is going to be here soon and I've still got to tong my hair.' Peanut and Little-Bit looked at each other. Mum put down the nail polish and turned to face the large mirror by the front door. 'I hope I pass muster. I've not been to the ballet for years.' She pulled her cheeks back towards her ears with her thumbs and index fingers. 'Now, where on earth is Leo? He was meant to be back ages ago. He promised me he'd walk the dog. Honestly, that brother of yours . . .'

The mere mention of Milton Stone's name had sent a chill down Peanut's spine. He was a partner at Mum's accountancy firm and, now that Dad was missing, it seemed like he wanted to be her boyfriend too. Not only that, but Peanut was certain that there was more to him than met the eye. She glanced up at the white fedora hanging on the coat hook that Mr Stone had left behind the last time he'd visited. A white fedora that, unfortunately, looked all too familiar.

3

Nerys and the Tickets

Peanut and Little-Bit left the house, shutting the bright yellow front door behind them. At the same time, Nerys, their mother's assistant at Blood, Stone & Partners, arrived at the gate at the other end of the path.

'Well, hello there, my lovelies. And where are you two going on this fine summer's evening?' The lilting, Welsh-accented voice danced out of her mouth and instantly made the world seem sunnier.

Little-Bit smiled. 'We're going to the National P—'

'We're going to the Science Museum!' interrupted Peanut. 'They do these really cool sleepovers in the school holidays where you get to look at stars and machines and, er, other sciencey things.'

'Ooh, I'm not gonna lie to you, that sounds wonderful.' She shut the gate behind her. 'Well, don't let me hold you up. Is your mother at home?'

'Yes,' sighed Peanut, suddenly remembering the likely purpose of Nerys's visit – to pick Mum up for her date with Mr Stone. 'She's just getting ready.'

'Tidy,' smiled Nerys, eyes twinkling mischievously. 'I've got her tickets here, and a little surprise to boot. Now, you have a lovely time at the museum. And don't do anything that might get you in trouble. I don't want to hear that you've been causing Mum any more grief.'

Peanut and Little-Bit said their goodbyes and walked through the gate on to Melody Road. A huge silver car was parked at the kerb, taking up at least two normal-sized spaces. An opaque black window slowly slid open to reveal a smiling middle-aged man wearing a dark-blue, peaked cap.

'Hello, Hammond,' said Peanut happily. 'How are things?'

'Mustn't grumble, young miss. Mustn't grumble,' said Blood, Stone & Partners' resident chauffeur. 'But I must say, it makes a nice change to see you. I have been doing so many airport runs recently. I dread to think how big sir's carbon footprint is.'

Peanut frowned. *So Stone is doing a lot of travelling, is he? What's he up to, I wonder?* Her suspicion-ometer had been working overtime recently.

'Hurry up, Peanut,' said Little-Bit, popping her sister's thought-balloon. 'Let's go and pick up Rockwell. We're late.'

Mrs Riley

The Rileys lived in Morse Tower, a block of flats ten minutes from Melody Road. Peanut and Little-Bit arrived on the seventh-floor landing, slightly out of breath, to find a tall, elegant lady in an amazing black-and-white-check cycling suit, wheeling a bike through the front door of 7C.

'Hello, girls,' she said cheerfully. 'Come in, come in. Shoes off please. ROCKWELL, YOUR FRIENDS ARE HERE!'

The sisters followed her through a small hallway and into a stylish living room. They sat on the sofa and thanked Rockwell's mum for the glasses of orange squash she handed them.

'So, you must be Peanut, and you must be Little-Bit.' She smiled a radiant smile. 'He talks about you all the time.'

'Likewise,' said Peanut. 'It's lovely to finally meet you, Mrs Riley.'

'Ooh, *Bridget*, please!' She sat on the chaise longue next to them. 'I'm so happy Rocky has made some friends at last. It hasn't been easy for him, you know. First, his dad and I split, and then he had to adapt to life at St Hubert's.'

Sounds familiar, thought Peanut.

'That stuff can be tough if you're sensitive like Rocky,' continued Bridget. 'He's a smart lad, and fairly happy with his own company, but he works so hard and he's such a worrier. Everybody needs friends of their own age to talk to, right?'

'I guess so,' said Little-Bit, 'although sometimes he talks a bit *too* much. Especially about homework and revision and stuff.'

Bridget and Peanut laughed.

Suddenly, a door next to the kitchen burst open, and a tall boy with even taller hair emerged with a big grin on his face. 'What's so funny?' he said.

'Well, it's definitely not that T-shirt!' said Peanut. Rockwell looked down at the big π symbol on his chest with the word 'Cutie' written in small type above it.

'Really?' A look of uncertainty flashed across his face, until he registered Peanut's teasing smile. 'Don't you think it's a good one for my nerdlinger fanbase?' he said. 'The mathmagicians at the, er, Science Museum are going to love it! Come on, let's get this show on the road, shall we?'

Peanut and Little-Bit stood up. 'Thanks for the drink, Mrs Riley. It was lovely to meet you.'

'You too, girls. Make sure you look after Rocky at the sleepover. Oh, and don't let him take things too seriously. Make sure he has a bit of fun!'

'Well, we'll do our best,' said Little-Bit, 'but it's hard to change the habits of a lifetime.'

5

The Northern Line

ocky?' Peanut laughed as they made their way to the tube station. 'Like the boxer? So do you do a bit of fighting in your spare time? Put 'em up, PUT 'EM UP!' She and her sister adopted their best Muhammad Ali stances and danced around in a circle pretending to throw punches.

'Very funny,' said Rockwell, shaking his head at their little charade. 'To be honest, I'm not sure you and Little Shrimp here are in a position to be taking the mickey out of anybody's nicknames.'

Fair point, thought Peanut, as the three of them went through the ticket barriers.

'So, did you hear the news?' she said when they

reached the Northern Line platform. 'About that painting in Spain?'

'Yeah. Another one bites the dust.' Rockwell hitched his rucksack further on to his shoulder. 'What was it called? *Guenevere*, wasn't it?'

Peanut shook her head. It never failed to amaze her just how little her friend knew about art.

'*Guernica*, by Picasso. And that's the tenth priceless work of art to disappear in less than three months.' She pulled a piece of paper from her dungarees pocket and unfolded it.

She shook her head. 'We shouldn't have left it so long before going back to Chroma. Maybe we could have saved some of those paintings if we'd returned sooner.'

'Oh, come on, you remember what happened the last time we were there,' said Rockwell. 'We came *this close* to being imprisoned forever by Mr White!' He held his finger and thumb a centimetre apart. 'We're lucky not to be locked up in the Spire right now, being guarded by RAZERs!'

The RAZERs, or Rigorous Attitude Zero Empathy Robots, formed the mechanical army used by Mr White to enforce his rule as Mayor of the City. There were thousands of them policing Chroma's citizens across the twelve districts. And Rockwell was correct: had it not been for Peanut's quick thinking, they would definitely still be imprisoned in the Spire right now. Luckily, they had managed to escape and, with the help of Mr and Mrs Markmaker, the leaders of the Resistance

movement against Mr White, return home safely to London. That had been the first time they'd used the top-secret Green Valleys portal which led to the National Portrait Gallery via a small hidden door behind a bust of Queen Victoria.

The tube train arrived at the platform with a rumble and the doors slid open accompanied by the familiar '*Mind the gap*' announcement.

'At least we know why White wanted your pencil so much,' said Rockwell as the three of them boarded and sat

down. 'He's obviously using it to travel between Chroma and the real world so that he can destroy all of the most-loved artworks on the planet.'

As the train lurched out of the station, Peanut thought back to the time she had sketched a picture of a door in her bedroom using Little Tail. It had turned out to be the portal that first led her to Chroma. That's when she'd discovered one of the pencil's most amazing powers: it was a magical portal-making device, a power totally unique to Little Tail. No wonder Mr White had looked so happy when he'd finally got his hands on it. He now had the ability to create doors between the two worlds wherever and whenever he liked.

'The thing that's confusing me,' said Peanut thoughtfully, 'is the way he is destroying the artworks. Disintegration. How would he even do that?'

The train's brakes screeched noisily as it pulled into the next station.

'Huh! It's obvious, isn't it?' said Little-Bit, not looking up from her copy of *2000 AD*.

'Is it?' said Peanut.

'Here we go,' sighed Rockwell. 'Come on then. Let's hear it, Sherlock.'

Little-Bit lowered her comic and looked at Rockwell.

'Well, Mr White must have made copies of the paintings and sculptures in Chroma and then, somehow, switched the fakes with the real things.'

Peanut and Rockwell frowned.

'Think about it,' continued Little-Bit. 'When you draw something in Chroma, it becomes real, right? And it stays real there. But whenever you draw something with Little Tail in our world, it crumbles away to dust as soon as someone touches it.'

'She's right,' said Peanut. 'Remember, Rockwell, when I drew that apple in the science lab at school to show you how the pencil worked? When you picked it up, it turned into that silvery grey powder.'

'Exactly,' said Little-Bit, 'And I bet it's the same with the magic stuff you draw in Chroma. If you were to bring something through to our world, a painting, for example, it would also disintegrate when touched.'

'*Mmmm*. I suppose . . .' said Rockwell. He seemed reluctant to admit that Little-Bit might be right.

'So if it is only the fake artworks that have been destroyed,' said Peanut, 'what's happened to the real ones?'

'Come on, surely even you two can work this out?' Little-Bit smiled, clearly enjoying herself now. 'I would bet my entire comic collection that he has stolen the originals for himself and is hiding them somewhere in the Illustrated City.'

A Surprise

Peanut spent the rest of the tube journey quietly mulling over Little-Bit's theory and concluded that it was pretty watertight. It was exciting to think that the great lost masterpieces may not be lost after all, and even more exciting to think that they might be able to find and return them.

Up until this point, she had mainly viewed the gang's trip back to Chroma as a fact-finding exercise (a) to determine whether Mr White was, as she suspected, behind the disappearing works of art, and (b) to find out why he did it. She was also keen to inform Mr and Mrs Markmaker, the leaders of the Resistance, of her suspicions about White's true identity. But now the purpose of the trip had changed. It had become a rescue mission, and she couldn't help but be a little thrilled by the prospect.

There was something else too. Peanut couldn't help but hope that there would be news of her dad. The Markmakers had told her that he had been working with the Resistance in secret for years, and that he had escaped from the Spire, but until now there had been no further information as to his whereabouts. Maybe this time someone would be able to tell her something.

'*THIS IS LEICESTER SQUARE,*' boomed the voice over the carriage speakers, bringing Peanut back into the real world with a jolt. '*CHANGE HERE FOR THE PICCADILLY LINE.*'

The three of them got off the train, made their way up the escalators and walked out into the balmy London evening. They picked their way through thirsty after-work crowds, and walked south along Charing Cross Road towards Trafalgar Square, passing the theatres, cafes, currency-exchange booths and chain restaurants. And there, next to a large statue of someone called Henry Irving, was the entrance to the National Portrait Gallery.

Peanut looked at her watch. 5.45 p.m. 'It closes in fifteen minutes. Perfect! It'll be emptying out nicely.'

The children dashed through the entrance doors, ran up the stairs to the first floor and turned right, following the signs to the Victorian Galleries.

QueenVictoria
Sir Joseph Edgar Boehm, 1st Bt.
Circa 1887

Then Peanut, who was leading the way, suddenly skidded to a halt.

'I don't believe it!' she said, aghast. 'Quick! Hide!'

But it was too late.

'Peanut?'

It was her older brother Leo! He was standing with a very tall security guard with huge shoulders, a neat white beard and a name badge that read 'Stanley'.

'Peanut, is that you?'

'Hi, Leo.'

'What are you doing here? Aren't you guys meant to be at the Science Museum?'

'What are *we* doing here? What are *you* doing here?' said Peanut. 'Since when have you visited art galleries? You don't like art. You like . . . maths!'

Leo, who was indeed a gifted mathematician, seemed taken aback. 'I . . . er . . . well . . . you see, I'm . . . trying to educate myself.' He ran his fingers through his messy red hair.

'I don't believe you.'

He sighed. 'Look. You want the truth?' He glanced at the security guard, who shook his head slightly. 'It's just that, I'm, er, embarrassed that I don't know more about this stuff. I'm nearly eighteen, after all. And so, well, here I am. To learn.'

'Rubbish!' snapped Peanut. 'I know you, Leonardo Jones, and I know full well that you have about as much interest in

Victorian portraiture as I do in . . . long division! No! As I do in FRACTIONS!'

Leo opened his mouth, but then closed it again, as if he had been about to say something but changed his mind at the last minute. Instead, he walked quietly to the other side of the gallery and stood looking at a large painting of a woman writing on some parchment with a quill.

Peanut went and stood next to him. She noticed that he looked tired.

'Leo,' she said softly. 'What's going on? Something's wrong. I know it. You haven't been the same since Dad disappeared. And now you're in an art gallery. An *art* gallery, Leo!'

'Do you know who this is, Peanut?' he said, looking up at the painting. 'It's Mary Shelley. She wrote *Frankenstein*. You know, that book about a bloke who built a big monster.'

Peanut nodded.

'Well, do you ever feel like *you've* created a monster? Y'know, when something just gets bigger and bigger, becomes more and more of a burden, until eventually you don't feel like you're in control of it any more?'

Peanut thought about Chroma and the Spire, Little Tail and Mr White. 'Yes,' she said. 'Sometimes I do.'

'Well, that's how I feel at the moment. It's all just getting a bit . . . much.'

'What is?' she said, putting a hand on his shoulder. 'Your A-level results?'

'A-level results?' He let out a short laugh, but then quickly composed himself. 'I mean, er, yes. A-level results. That's it. I'm worried about my A-level results.'

Peanut's eyes narrowed. Something didn't quite ring true.

'Listen, Peanut, I've got to go home. I'm already late. Don't worry, I won't tell Mum that I saw you here.'

'Thanks.'

He turned to look along the gallery, towards a small bust of Queen Victoria at the far end of the room, and then looked back at his sister. 'Peanut, promise me one thing. Whatever it is that you're up to, you will be careful.'

'Er, and what, exactly, do you think I'm up to?' She also shot a look to Queen Victoria.

'Just promise me, OK?'

Peanut nodded. 'OK, I promise.'

'Thank you.'

He ruffled her topknot, went over to say goodbye to

Little-Bit and Rockwell, then walked towards the exit. 'I'll see you when you get back,' he called over his shoulder.

And that's when she noticed it.

Something small and yellow sticking out of the back pocket of his jeans. Something that looked remarkably like a Post-it note.

7
Get Back

As Stanley, the security guard with the white beard, was ushering the last remaining visitors towards the stairs, he turned back to look at Peanut, Rockwell and Little-Bit, who were lingering by the portrait of Mary Shelley.

'LADIES AND GENTLEMAN. PLEASE MAKE YOUR WAY TOWARDS THE EXIT. THE GALLERY IS NOW CLOSED.'

Again, it seemed to Peanut that he held their gaze for a beat or two longer than seemed normal. And then he disappeared around the corner.

The children were completely alone.

'Now's our chance!' said Rockwell. 'Come on!'

The three of them ran across the parquet floor and came skidding to a halt in front of Queen Victoria. The white marble bust sat nobly on a tall wooden plinth, the statue's eye-level meeting Peanut's exactly.

'She doesn't look very happy today,' said Peanut.

'If I were Queen,' said Little-Bit, 'you wouldn't ever be able to get the smile off my face!'

'Rockwell. The door,' said Peanut.

He knelt, reached behind the plinth and patted the wall down, feeling for the tiny handle. The portal was very cleverly hidden, the edges of the door virtually invisible unless you looked really closely. The only tell-tale sign that anything was out of the ordinary was the fact that there were

a couple of old, dry oak leaves on the floor.

'Found it!'

He pulled the secret door as far open as he could. 'You first, Peanut. See you on the other side . . .'

Peanut squeezed into the narrow gap between the plinth and the wall, and dived head first through the portal, closely followed by Little-Bit and, finally, Rockwell, who closed it behind them.

Slowly, they made their way along the low, leafy passageway, all three of them bent double at first but walking more and more upright with each step.

'It's like that March of Progress image,' said Rockwell, chuckling. 'You know, the Ascent of Man!'

41

'Dude, you really need to update your references,' said Peanut, shaking her head.

The further they went, the wider and taller the passageway became. After a few minutes, Little-Bit stopped walking and cocked an ear skyward.

'Can you hear that?'

'What?' said Rockwell.

'That music.'

Sure enough, a beautiful melody was drifting through the branches above their heads. It swirled around the leaves as it dipped and soared, and sounded as if it were being played by an airborne version of the Royal Philharmonic's woodwind section.

When the children reached the end of the passage, all three of them looked up towards the sound. And there, tracing wide circles high above the trees, were three old friends.

8
The Green Valleys

'Kaleidoscoppi!' said Peanut, beaming at the beautiful birds, one gold-crested, one red and one green, as they carved elegant shapes through the sky, their long feathery trains following like kite tails.

Kaleidoscoppi were native to Chroma and were said to have the power to inspire amazing ideas in whoever hears their song. Mr White had, of course, ordered their capture and extermination many years ago, but a lucky few still flew free.

Suddenly, the gold-crested bird broke away and swooped down towards the mesmerised children, arriving with a rush of air. He hovered in front of Peanut and sang a few bars of his beautiful melody before shooting back up to join the others and leading them in a westerly direction.

'I think they want us to follow them,' said Peanut.

The early evening sun shone over the undulating wolds of the Green Valleys, gilding the patchwork of emerald, lime and ochre fields. Peanut, who had taken the bandolier from her bag and was now proudly wearing it, painted watercolour parasols for herself, Rockwell and Little-Bit. Keeping a careful eye out for patrolling RAZERs, the children followed the kaleidoscoppi as they swooped and soared between the candyfloss clouds.

After an hour or so, they found themselves walking along the banks of a winding ribbon of water which sliced through the lush countryside. Over the next thirty minutes, the river's pace slowed as the twists and turns became sharper, and it was almost still by the time they arrived at a pretty red-and-white brick mill situated on a very tight curve.

'Wow,' said Peanut.

'It's so beautiful,' said Little-Bit.

'It reminds me of one of those boxes of chocolates that I get from the petrol station for Mum on Mother's Day,' said Rockwell, not quite managing to embrace the romance of the scene.

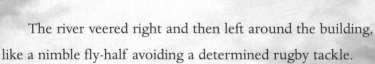

The river veered right and then left around the building, like a nimble fly-half avoiding a determined rugby tackle. At this point on its journey, the water was only around thirty centimetres deep, a fact made more obvious by the large wooden wagon sitting, abandoned, right in the middle of the river. Someone had obviously attempted to pull the hay wain from one bank to the other and given up halfway.

As they flew over the wagon, the three kaleidoscoppi suddenly moved into a narrow circle formation, descended helter-skelter-style and landed on the riverbank.

They looked directly at the approaching children and sang an impossibly beautiful verse before nodding their heads and taking off again.

'Thank you,' whispered Peanut as the great birds disappeared towards the horizon.

'What now?' asked Little-Bit, looking around.

'You don't think the new Bunker could be near here, do you?' said Rockwell. 'Hang on. I think there's something on that cart.'

'Some*thing*, or some*one*?' said Peanut.

Sure enough, standing on the hay wain and looking straight at them was a small scribble of fur with legs and a tail. And it was wagging its tail so hard that the entire wagon was swaying from side to side.

Doodle and the Wagon

'OODLE!' shouted Little-Bit, before splashing out across the water and flinging her arms around the dog she'd waited so long to see.

Doodle had been the gang's constant companion throughout their first adventure in Chroma and belonged to the Markmakers. He raced back and forth between Little-Bit, Rockwell and Peanut, as if he couldn't decide who he was most happy to see.

'Hello, boy!' said Peanut, ruffling the soft charcoal fur around the dog's neck as he wagged his tail excitedly. 'It's great to see you too!'

'If Doodle's here, that must mean the Markmakers aren't far away,' said Rockwell, trying to avoid the dog's enthusiastic attempts to lick his face. 'Maybe that old mill over there is their new HQ?'

Peanut looked over at the building and shook her head. 'Too conspicuous for a secret bunker,' she said. 'My gut tells me we're looking for something a bit more subtle.'

'Maybe there's a door in one of those tree trunks,' said Little-Bit, pointing to the large oaks on the far bank beyond the mill. 'Or under one of those hay-bales in the field.'

'What about *that*?' said Rockwell, pointing. Right in the middle of the cart, bolted to the platform, was a backplate holding a heavy-looking metal ring. 'It looks just like the handle of the hatch that led to the Bunker back in the North Draw.'

'I think Rocky is right,' said Little-Bit.

All three of them climbed up on to the cart and grabbed the ring. They pulled as hard as they could, and, sure enough, a section of the wagon's floor started to lift up like a trapdoor. When it reached a vertical position, something clicked and it stayed upright. The children looked down through the opening, and where they might have expected to see water flowing beneath the cart, they saw instead a staircase which seemed to lead deep into the river.

'Cool!' exclaimed Little-Bit, as Doodle jumped through the opening. 'Looks like we're going underwater!'

10
The Bunker, Mark II

he four of them made their way down the
long flight of stairs and found themselves in a
bright, circular room with three large openings
cut into the wall. Above the one on the left was a sign saying
'Arsenal' written in bright pink handwriting, above the middle
one it said 'Transport' in bright blue, and above the one on
the right it said 'Map Room' in pink. Peanut, Rockwell and
Little-Bit dutifully followed Doodle through the one marked
'Arsenal'.

'WHOA!' exclaimed Rockwell. 'This is INCREDIBLE!'

In front of them, laid out on the floor and arranged
with military precision, were row upon row of art materials:
weapons ready to do battle in Mr White's attack on creativity.

There were pens, pencils, crayons, pastels, paints, paintbrushes, palette knives, jars of ink, cans of spray paint, and much, much more, all grouped by type, and all hand-drawn in either bright pink or bright blue pencil. They filled the brightly lit, high-ceilinged room, which Peanut reckoned was about the same

size as the sports hall at Melody High. There must have been
hundreds of thousands of items.

'Isn't it amazing what a couple of old pencils can produce?' said a friendly voice from behind them.

The three children spun around to see a small lady with snow-white hair piled up into a neat bun, and a pair of very large, black-rimmed glasses perched on the end of her nose. She was holding two ancient-looking pencils, one bright pink and one bright blue.

'MRS M!' all three of them cried in unison, before enveloping her in a group hug.

'Oh, it's lovely to see you again,' said Millicent Markmaker, pushing the pencils into her hair bun, 'I'm so glad you're back! I trust you kept safe and didn't run into any trouble on your way here?'

'Yes!' said Peanut, 'We didn't see a single RAZER.'

'Thank goodness!' said Mrs M. 'Especially as I see you have a new bandolier! I love it. Practical, hardwearing, yet *très chic*. Bravo, young lady, bravo!'

'So did you draw all of these?' asked Little-Bit. Her eyes grew wide as she surveyed the thousands of items in front of them.

'Teamwork makes the dream work, my dear,' said Mrs M.

'The little production line that we started the last time you were here has gone from strength to strength, and, as you can see, we have built up quite the arsenal. One hopes one won't need to go into battle, but I fear that is inevitable now if Chroma is to survive.'

'Where's Mr M?' said Rockwell. 'Is he here too?'

'He certainly is. Shall we go and see him?'

They left the Arsenal and walked through the door marked 'Transport'. This room was just as cavernous, but much, much busier. Lots of people, all armed with pink and blue art equipment, were buzzing around the many large vehicles that filled the hall. There were jeeps, trucks, lorries, tanks, hovercraft and helicopters. Immediately to their right, a tall woman wearing a headscarf was painstakingly colouring in the tread on the tyres of a large armoured car, while a very cute unicorn was sitting on top of it painting the gun turret.

'He must be from the Cute Quarter,' said Rockwell, nodding towards the unicorn. The children knew from first-hand experience that not everything from the Cute Quarter was as adorable as it looked. He shivered at the memory of Lulu Kawaii, an evil robotic panda they had encountered the last time they were there.

'Ah! There you are!' A very smiley man, wearing glasses similar to Mrs M's, had popped his head out of the hatch. 'Great to see you all again.'

'Hi, Mr M,' said Peanut.

'Wow! You guys have been BUSY!'

'Yes, well, it's very much a case of "seize the moment", I'm afraid,' he replied. 'Who knows how long my wife will manage to keep her old pencils away from Mr White's clutches.'

He heaved himself out and, very nimbly for a man in his seventies, jumped down from the car.

'Right then. Who fancies a cup of tea? We have a lot of catching up to do.'

The Map Room

Peanut, Rockwell, Little-Bit, Mr Markmaker, Mrs Markmaker and Doodle walked out into the lobby and through the door marked 'Map Room'. It led to a small antechamber which resembled an airport security checkpoint. It was being marshalled by three cartoon gorillas wearing blue uniforms and peaked caps. Unsmiling, they guided the group through the full-body scanners, baggage screening (Peanut had to remove her bandolier) and the biometric identification tests, before opening another door at the far end and grumpily waving them through.

It led to a dimly lit, perfectly circular chamber the size of a small circus tent. Despite being considerably smaller than the hangars they'd already visited, it was no less impressive. It was dominated by a huge table, about five metres in diameter, on which was printed a massive version of the map of Chroma that Mrs M had given Peanut during her first visit – the one that was safely folded up in the pocket of Peanut's dungarees.

Dotted around the various city districts were lots of miniature pink and blue models of the vehicles that they'd seen in the Transport Room. There were also several tiny model RAZER platoons, five long sticks with felt blocks on the end, and, right in the centre, a two metre-tall, white, needle-shaped tower, dotted with a spiral of tiny black windows. The infamous Spire. This was surrounded by seven concentric

circles, painted red, orange, yellow, green, blue, indigo and violet, to represent the Rainbow Lake, the magical body of water at the heart of the city. It was said that a single swim in the lake had the power to boost a person's creativity to ten times its normal level. Peanut and the gang had swum through it on their last adventure, and she had definitely noticed an improvement in her drawing skills ever since.

'It's a war room!' said Rockwell. 'Just like the ones they had in those old films about World War Two! COOL!'

'We call it the Map Room,' said Mrs M, 'but yes, it does serve a very similar purpose. It's where we plan our Resistance activity against Mr White.' She flicked a switch on the wall, and a raft of spotlights in the ceiling lit the map up like a theatre stage, and large illuminated letters indicated north, south, east and west on the circular wall.

Rockwell nodded appreciatively.

'Right, teas all round then,' said Mr M, before disappearing through a triangular door to their left.

'And biscuits?' said Little-Bit hopefully.

'I think I might have some chocolate ones hidden away somewhere,' said Mr M, giving the little girl a wink.

'So,' said Peanut. 'What can we do to help? We've worked out, or rather LB's worked out, that Mr White must be stealing masterpieces from all over the world.'

'My goodness. That does sound like him,' said Mrs M. She sat down on one of the chairs at the table. 'We both have so much news to share. First, let me tell you what's been happening in Chroma since you were last here.'

The three children took a seat as Mr M emerged through the triangular doorway with a tray full of steaming mugs and a plate of chocolate biscuits. He handed them out and sat down next to Little-Bit.

'So, while we have been working on ours, White has bolstered his own arsenal with a speed that we couldn't have

imagined,' continued Mrs M. 'The first thing, or things, to tell you about are these.'

She reached under the table and pulled out a model of a vehicle, about thirty centimetres wide, and drawn in blue pencil.

'I recognise that,' said Peanut.

'It's the Big X,' said Little-Bit.

'It certainly is,' said Mrs M. She placed it on the map and used one of the sticks with the felt blocks to push it towards the centre, carefully positioning it in the narrowest area of Modernia. She then spun it around until it faced south.

The Big X was the huge, monstrous machine that had been built by Mr White to 'mono' the city – to rid it of all its colour. It had the capacity to move relentlessly forward on its giant tracks and chew up everything in its path, leaving a black, white and grey wasteland in its wake. The children had come face to face with it once before, and it wasn't an experience any of them would particularly like to repeat.

Mrs M reached under the table again and pulled out another model, exactly the same as the first. This time she placed it in the Grid, again facing outwards. Then she pulled out another, which she placed in Cubeside. Another in Warholia. Then Dali Point West. Then the Green Valleys. In fact, she kept producing them, like a magician pulling rabbit after rabbit from a hat, until twelve Big Xs sat in a circle at the centre of the map, all of them facing menacingly outwards and pointing towards each of Chroma's districts. Doodle whimpered, and jumped on to Little-Bit's lap.

'Twelve Big Xs! One was terrifying enough,' gasped Peanut. 'He's going to mono the entire city, isn't he?'

12
A Rather Beautiful Mystery

think I need to lie down,' said Rockwell, tiny beads of sweat appearing on his brow.

'I know how you feel,' smiled Mrs M, looking fondly at Rockwell. 'And yes, Peanut, monoing the entire city has always been part of his plan, but twelve Big Xs would mean he could make it happen much quicker than we ever thought possible.'

'*Part* of his plan?' said Peanut, 'Surely, once the whole of Chroma is monoed, that's game over, isn't it? What else could he possibly want to achieve?'

'Actually, we think he wants to ensure that no one from

your world can *ever* visit our city again,' said Mr M gravely.

'I don't understand,' said Little-Bit as she scratched Doodle under the chin. 'Why would he care who comes to Chroma, if he's going to mono everything anyway?'

'Well,' said Mrs M, removing her glasses. 'Do you remember that I told you that most of your world's great creatives have visited Chroma at some point? That they have swum in the Rainbow Lake and, in some cases, spent a great deal of time here? And, while it's true that the lake boosted their creativity and helped them to become great artists, we shouldn't forget that in return, they brought their own special talent to the Illustrated City. They left their mark. A few even had entire districts named after them.'

'For example –' she pointed to an area on the map marked 'Vincent Fields' – 'a Dutch chap named Van Gogh was responsible for the look of much of this area.'

'And over here –' Mr M gestured to the narrow district at nine o'clock on the map marked 'Dali Point West' – 'young Salvador had great fun. What an imagination! A total one-off!'

'Well, we think White wants to stop that happening,' said Mrs M. 'He doesn't want anybody creative visiting the city.'

'Right. So how did, er . . . *do* they all get here?' asked Little-Bit.

'Well,' continued Mrs M, 'that has always been one of the great and enduring mysteries of Chroma. I mean, we already knew about at least one secret gateway between your world and ours, thanks to your daddy.'

'The Green Valleys portal,' said Peanut, her cheeks flushing with pride, as she thought of Dad going through the very same doorway that she, Little-Bit and Rockwell had gone through only a few hours earlier.

'That's right, my dear,' said Mrs M, smiling. 'Gary was

one of our first and best recruits to the Resistance movement against Mr White. He did indeed reveal that gateway to us. We always suspected there were others, there had to be, but we never knew where they were. Not that anybody looked very hard – we citizens of Chroma had no need of a portal, after all. And the whole visiting-artists thing was always considered a rather beautiful mystery. These amazing people would appear out of nowhere, swim in the lake, produce their amazing art, and then off they'd go, having left their mark on our city. It was a win-win situation.'

'The thing is, while artists continue to find their way to Chroma, tiny seeds of their talent will find a way to grow here – no matter how much Mr White tries to mono the city,' said Mr M. 'It's a system that's been working for centuries. So the only way he could totally destroy Chroma would be to stop creatives coming.'

'Yes,' said Mrs M darkly, as she put her glasses back on. 'That would break the system beyond all repair.'

13
FridaDaDa

r M stood up and started to walk slowly around the giant map.

'We knew that White himself was not from Chroma and must be using a portal to travel between the two worlds. So Gary and several other brave Resistance operatives were given top-secret spying missions. They were charged with keeping an eye on White's movements and working out where he was going. That's when they discovered the portal. Once we knew he was travelling between Chroma and London, we thought that if we could discover his identity in your world, maybe we could put a stop to the damage that he was inflicting upon ours.'

Peanut and Rockwell shot each other a knowing look.

'And then, about six years ago, just before your first visit to Chroma, something odd started to happen,' said Mrs M.

'Six years ago?' said Rockwell.

'Remember, Rocky,' said Little-Bit, 'time moves at a different speed in Chroma. About twenty-four times faster, to be exact.'

'Go on,' said Peanut, looking wide-eyed at Mrs M. 'You were saying something odd started to happen?'

'That's right. Resistance members secretly tracking White reported that he was making regular journeys, accompanied by a platoon of RAZERs and Alan, his big oaf of a sidekick, from the Spire to the city limits.' She stood up and walked left around the table. 'To this place, right at the very edge of Warholia. They made the exact same return trip more than thirty times over a six-month period.'

Mr M went and stood next to his wife. 'We began to suspect that they had discovered another portal.'

'The thing is,' continued Mrs M, 'White himself always returned from these trips alongside the RAZERs and Alan. We assumed that if he had found a portal, he would use it. But he didn't seem to, so we could never be a hundred per cent sure that he'd discovered anything.'

Mr M nodded in agreement. 'Meanwhile, other members of the Resistance began to notice that the water levels in the Rainbow Lake were dropping. Very slowly – only a few millimetres each month – but dropping nevertheless. In fact, it is now *fifty centimetres* shallower than it was ten years ago. And considering the size of the lake, that means a heck of a lot of our very special water has vanished.'

'All of these strange happenings meant that we were very keen to know what White was up to at all times. Now, as you know, dear Gary had been missing for some time by then, so we put our next best surveillance operative on the case.' Mrs M paused and looked at her husband. 'Frida DaDa.'

'Frida DaDa?' exclaimed Rockwell.

'The very same.' Mrs M looked over to the wall at a picture of a square-jawed woman with dark, intense eyes set beneath a heavy brow.

'Oh,' said Peanut, eyes shining with hope. 'Where is she? If she works on the same mission that my dad did, maybe she knows something that could lead us to him? We'd love to talk to her.'

'I wish you could,' said Mrs M. 'Unfortunately, she disappeared just after you left Chroma.'

14

The Factory Vent and the Tin of Soup

'Oh no! What happened?' said Peanut.

Mrs M took a deep breath and steeled herself.

'Well, as I said, Frida was our best available agent. When it comes to covert surveillance there are few finer.'

'As cunning as a fox and as stealthy as a jaguar,' said Mr M, a note of pride in his voice.

'She'd been tracking White for a long, long time,' continued Mrs M. 'In fact it was Frida who reported back on many of his original visits out to Warholia. After he stole Little Tail from you, however, those trips suddenly stopped. For a while at least.'

Peanut bristled at the thought of that man being in possession of the magical pencil. *Her* magical pencil. 'For a while?' she said.

'Yes. Until a year after you last visited, in fact.' Her voice caught in her throat and she pulled a handkerchief from her sleeve.

'Oh, Millicent,' said Mr M, 'don't upset yourself. It's not your fault.'

'But I can't help feeling responsible, Malcolm,' she replied, dabbing at her eyes.

'Listen,' he said. 'Frida knew the risks. She knew what she'd signed up for.'

'So what happened?' asked Rockwell.

'She was at her regular post overlooking the Spire,' said Mrs M, 'when she saw Mr White, a platoon of RAZERs and Alan leave and head towards Warholia, just as they'd done many times before. So Frida followed them, at a safe distance, to the same place that they always used to visit – a small alleyway at the side of one of the old factories in the industrial zone. But, this time, things were different.'

'How so?' asked Peanut.

'Well, a couple of minutes after arriving, the RAZERS and Alan turned right around and headed back to the Spire. *Without* White.'

'He must have gone through a portal!' gasped Little-Bit.

Mr M nodded. 'Frida immediately radioed in to tell us what had happened, and to ask whether she should investigate further.'

'I was on the other end of that radio,' sniffed Mrs M, 'and I was the one that said she should.'

Mr M put an arm around his wife. 'Which *was* the right call. We'd been tracking him for years by this point. It was our breakthrough moment, so *of course* she had to investigate further.'

'So did she go and have a look down the alleyway?' asked Rockwell.

'She did. And, unsurprisingly, found that it was totally empty.' Mr M glanced over at his wife. 'But Frida did notice something. A small air vent, a metre or so from the floor, with its front panel slightly ajar.'

'She went through it, didn't she?' said Little-Bit.

'Indeed she did.'

'And where did it lead?'

'It led,' said Mr M, 'to MoMA, the Museum of Modern

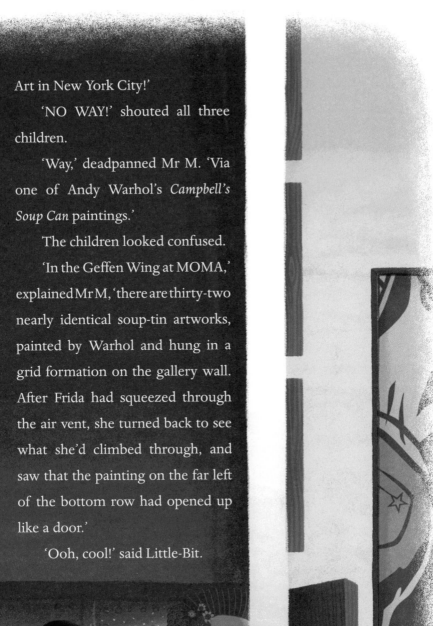

Art in New York City!'

'NO WAY!' shouted all three children.

'Way,' deadpanned Mr M. 'Via one of Andy Warhol's *Campbell's Soup Can* paintings.'

The children looked confused.

'In the Geffen Wing at MOMA,' explained Mr M, 'there are thirty-two nearly identical soup-tin artworks, painted by Warhol and hung in a grid formation on the gallery wall. After Frida had squeezed through the air vent, she turned back to see what she'd climbed through, and saw that the painting on the far left of the bottom row had opened up like a door.'

'Ooh, cool!' said Little-Bit.

'So did she then follow Mr White through New York?' asked Peanut.

'That's the thing. We don't know,' said Mrs M, her voice thick with emotion. 'The last we heard from her was when she radioed to tell us about MoMA and the painting. She said she was going to investigate further, but the connection went dead soon afterwards.'

'So she didn't come back through the portal later on?'

'Unfortunately not. Of course, we sent backup to Warholia immediately, but by the time the agents arrived, the vent in the factory wall was . . . just a vent in a factory wall.'

'What do you mean?' said Peanut.

'It didn't lead anywhere,' said Mr M. 'The portal had, somehow, been . . . closed.'

Doodle, still sitting on Little-Bit's lap, whimpered quietly.

Mrs M shook her head. 'Which meant that Frida DaDa couldn't get back to Chroma. And she hasn't been seen since.'

15
The Eleven Portals

'So she's trapped in New York?' said Peanut.

'It seems likely,' sighed Mrs M, 'I just hope she's OK. We hope to find a way to bring her back one day.'

'And what about Mr White? Did he come back?'

'Well, that's the curious thing,' said Mr M. 'Another Resistance operative spotted him less than an hour later back at the Spire.'

'Less than an hour?' said Rockwell. 'How is that even possible?'

'Well, don't forget that by this time White had Conté's pencil in his possession. And, as you know, the great power of Pencil Number One is that it can draw portals between the worlds.'

'So we think White drew a new portal that led to the Spire, and he simply walked back through,' said Mrs M. 'Gosh, Conté really knew what he was doing when he invented that thing!'

'What happened next?' asked Rockwell.

'Well, we carried on with our surveillance,' said Mr M. 'We owed it to Frida not to give up. Millicent and I even went on a few of the reconnaissance mission ourselves.'

'And did you discover anything else?' said Peanut.

'Yes.' Mrs M nodded. 'Quite a lot actually. Over the next few months, White and his cronies started to make more trips to the city limits. And this time, he didn't stick to Warholia. He visited pretty much every district. First it was Vincent Fields, then the Grid, then Modernia. In fact, he worked his way around the entire city. Well, *almost* the entire city.'

'We should mention that he visited each district twice,' chimed in Mr M. 'The first trip must have always been a recce, of sorts, because after a few hours combing the city limits, he returned to the Spire alongside the RAZERs and Alan. Then they would all head back out in a much more targeted way a day or two later. And this time, crucially, the RAZERs and Alan would return to the Spire without White. The pattern was always the same.'

'So he must have discovered more portals!' gasped Little-Bit.

'That's right, little one,' said Mrs M.

'But, fortunately, we *also* discovered them!' added Mr M. 'You see, Frida isn't our only surveillance expert. As Mr White found each portal and disappeared through them, one of our agents would be watching, and they would follow him a few minutes later when the coast was clear. They were under strict instructions to simply observe their surroundings, try to get a sense of where in the world they were, and come straight back through the portal as quickly as possible. We didn't want any repeats of what happened to Frida.'

'And were your agents able to tell where each portal led?' asked Rockwell.

'They were. We've managed to compile a pretty comprehensive list.' She handed a piece of paper to Peanut.

'Whoa!' said Peanut. 'So the portals lead to places all over the world?'

'Apparently so,' said Mrs M.

① **Warholia**
Campbell's Soup Can painting ← WARHOL
MUSEUM OF MODERN ART, NEW YORK, USA

② **Dali Point West** **Mae West Lips Sofa** ← DALI
DALI THEATRE and MUSEUM, SPAIN

③ **The Green Valleys**
Bust of Queen Victoria ← BOEHM
NATIONAL PORTRAIT GALLERY, LONDON, ENGLAND

④ **The Ink District** **Qingming Shanghetu** ← ZHANG ZEDUAN
PALACE MUSEUM, THE FORBIDDEN CITY, BEIJING, CHINA

⑤ **The Strip**
Colorado Nursery Wall ← SCHULZ
CHARLES M SCHULZ MUSEUM, SANTA ROSA, USA

⑥ **The Light District**
Dining Room fireplace
MONET'S HOUSE, GIVERNY, FRANCE

⑦ **Vincent Field**
Sunflowers painting ← VAN GOGH
VAN GOGH MUSEUM, AMSTERDAM, HOLLAND

⑧ **Die Brücke** **Under the bed at Munch's House**
ÅSGÅRDSTRAND, NORWAY

⑨ **Modernia**
Guernica painting ← PICASSO
MUSEO REINA SOFIA, MADRID, SPAIN

⑩ **The Grid**
Composition II in Red, ← MONDRIAN
Blue & Yellow painting
KUNSTHAUS, ZURICH, SWITZERLAND

⑪ **Eubeside - La Pleureuse** ← FRANCOISE-XAVIER
and CLAUDE LALANNE
HAKONE OPEN-AIR MUSEUM, JAPAN

⑫ **The North Draw**

'Hang on a second.' Peanut pulled the map, with her handwritten list of missing artworks on the back, from her dungarees pocket. 'MoMA, the Forbidden City, the Van Gogh Museum – this tallies almost perfectly with the missing masterpieces. The ones that have been mysteriously disintegrating. Apart from the National Portrait Gallery, these are the exact places they disappeared from!'

'I wondered if they might be,' said Mrs M.

'We were sure that Mr White must be stealing the artworks! Little-Bit worked out that, somehow, he must be making fakes here in Chroma, and replacing the originals. Then he probably brings the originals back here. I bet he's got them all stored somewhere in the Spire.'

'Quite possibly,' said Mrs M, 'and we will do our best to recover them.'

'That's outrageous!' said Rockwell. 'I wish we could just arrest him or something.'

'Well, that could be a bit tricky due to the whole army-of-robots thing,' said Mr M.

'To be honest,' said Mrs M, 'I think that the stealing of the artworks is a bit of a red herring. I'd wager that it's just a little distraction to keep him amused while he concentrates on his masterplan.'

'His masterplan?' said Rockwell, nervousness creeping into his voice.

'Yes. You see, when we sent agents back to the location of each portal a few hours after White went through them, on every single occasion the portal no longer worked. It had been closed. Just like that vent in Warholia,' said Mr M.

'And you think Mr White did that?' asked Peanut.

'We do.'

'So his masterplan is . . . to close all of the portals?'

'Yes. No portals means no creatives. And that would mean the end of the Illustrated City,' said Mrs M.

'So do you see why we must fight back?' said Mr M. 'We have to stop him.'

Stanley

'I have a question.' Peanut was looking at Mrs M. 'Why is there nothing written next to the North Draw? Has he not found a portal there yet?'

'Well spotted! As I said earlier, he has worked his way around *almost* the entire city. If there is a twelfth portal in the North Draw, which we suspect there must be, he has yet to travel through it. He has, however, already carried out a recce there. Yesterday, in fact. We are expecting him to take another little trip to its outskirts any day now. Our agents are primed and ready to follow him.'

'Also, what about the Green Valleys portal?' said Little-Bit, 'The one we just came through from the National Portrait Gallery? Why hasn't he closed that one yet?'

'Yeah. I assume he doesn't need to use it any more,' said Peanut.

'No, he doesn't. We suspect he's keeping it open as a kind of safety net, just in case anything happens to the pencil before his mission to destroy Chroma is complete.'

'But why keep that particular one open when he's got rid of all the others?' asked Rockwell.

'Do you remember Peanut's dad's top-secret spying mission that I mentioned earlier?' said Mrs M.

'Dad's mission?' said Peanut. 'The one where he had to find out Mr White's identity and where he was travelling to?'

'That's the one. If you recall, I said that he had been working with other Resistance operatives.'

The children nodded.

'Well, one of those operatives is still in place and has been working undercover at the National Portrait Gallery for many years now.'

'Ooooh, really?' said Rockwell, cheering up a bit. 'Who is it? Are they in disguise?'

'Are they dressed as the bust of Queen Victoria?' said a gleeful Little-Bit. 'Is it just a person pretending to be a statue, like those people in Covent Garden?'

'Ha!' said Mrs M. 'I think even the best mime in the world might struggle to keep still for that long. No, our operative works in the gallery as a security guard. It's the perfect cover.'

Something stirred in Peanut's memory. 'Hang on, his name's not Stanley, is it?'

'Why, yes,' said Mr M, his eyebrows raised. 'Have you met him then?'

'Kind of. I, er, had a feeling there might have been more to him than met the eye.' Peanut suddenly remembered seeing Stanley talking to her brother earlier that day. *So what was that about?* she thought.

'Well, Stanley has confirmed that White has not been through the Green Valleys portal at all since Pencil Number One came into his possession,' said Mrs M. 'Which is interesting, given where we think he might be travelling to in London.'

'In London?' said Peanut, suddenly more upright. 'You mean, you know exactly where he goes when he leaves Chroma?' She looked over at Rockwell.

'Yes. Your dad and Stanley were doing such a brilliant job of tracking White. They were on the verge of a breakthrough when Gary was imprisoned. Terrible timing.'

'What had they discovered?' asked Peanut.

'They'd tracked him to his workplace in London. They were almost certain that . . .' Mrs M paused. 'Now, Peanut, Little-Bit, I don't want to frighten you, but . . .'

Peanut stood. 'Where did they track him to?'

'To Blood, Stone & Partners,' said Mrs M. 'Your mother's accountancy firm.'

17
The Fedora

eanut and Rockwell looked at each other.

'Tell them,' said Rockwell.

'Tell us what?' asked Mr M. 'Peanut, do you know something?'

'Maybe,' said Peanut, sitting back down. 'I, er . . . I think I might know who Mr White is. And I think you've just confirmed it.'

'Go on,' said Mrs M gently.

'I think – *we* think – he's Milton Stone. My mum's boss.'

Rockwell nodded enthusiastically.

Mrs M looked anxious. 'OK. Why do you think that?'

Peanut shuffled in her seat. 'Well, first of all, he's pretty much the same height as Mr White. Secondly, Mr Stone is horrible and Mr White is also horrible. Thirdly, he has a very similar turn of phrase. For example, they both said something to me about paper not growing on trees.'

'They are wrong of course,' said Little-Bit, 'because, technically, paper does grow on trees. Sure, you have to turn the raw wood into pulp first and mix in a few chemicals, maybe a caustic soda and some sodium sulphide, a dash of hypochlorite for bleaching, and obviously some epichlorohydrin to strengthen—'

'All right, Brainiac,' interrupted Rockwell. 'We get it. You know a lot of stuff. But try and keep a lid on it for a second if you can. Go on, Peanut, tell them about the thing. You know, the clincher. The irrefutable proof.'

'OK.' Peanut took a deep breath. 'He's also got a white fedora. It looks exactly the same as Mr White's.'

'Hmmm,' said Mr M, frowning. 'If you're right, Peanut, this is a really worrying development. Your family could be in danger. White, er . . . Stone knows you've been to Chroma. He knows you had Pencil Number One. Which must mean he knows . . .' He looked over at his wife.

'. . . that Peanut's dad might be Conté's heir,' they said together.

18
Conté's Heir

'onté's heir?' said Peanut. 'What do you mean?'

'Ever since we first met in that cosy old bunker,' said Mrs M, 'and you showed me Pencil Number One, Little Tail as you call it, I've wondered how it came to be in your father's possession. The world's first pencil, hand-crafted by the great Nicolas-Jacques Conté himself. An almost mythological object. And you found it at the bottom of a box full of Post-it notes. Just incredible.'

'It really is,' agreed her husband. 'Children, you do realise that this pencil is legendary in Chroma, don't you? And, as such, there have always been lots of stories associated with it. Fairy tales, I suppose you'd call them.'

'My parents would tell me them at bedtime,' said Mrs M,

her cheeks reddening. 'One night, the pencil might turn into a sword used to fight dragons. The next, a powerful oar to row across vast oceans. Then, it would be a magic wand to battle wizards . . .'

'A pencil *is* a wand,' said Peanut. 'Any pencil. I've always thought that. Every single one has magic inside it.'

'But this one, as you know, has *actual* magic inside it. And a very special kind of magic too,' said Mrs M. 'Nobody was ever really sure what form that magic took, hence all the wildly varying stories, but now we know.' She was smiling and shaking her head in disbelief. 'Now we *actually* know.'

'It was also said,' added Mr M, 'that when Conté himself wielded the pencil, it became even more powerful. It unleashed a creative force so potent that it could paint the heavens with rainbows and fill the oceans with colour. One of my favourite stories tells how Conté painted the entire Spire just by pointing Pencil Number One at it. Ribbons and ribbons of beautiful kaleidoscopic colour just poured from the tip, apparently.'

'Oh, how I wish you children could have seen the tower before it was whitewashed by You Know Who,' said Mrs M. 'It was *the* most beautiful sight.'

'Legend has it,' said Mr M, 'that as the pencil was handed down from generation to generation, Conté's heirs inherited his power. And that when they came of age and used Little Tail, incredible things would also happen.'

'Hang on! Why has it passed into legend?' said Rockwell. 'Surely there is some evidence of this stuff happening?'

'Not really. In fact there is no official record of the pencil's existence at all. Also, back in Conté's day, family records tended to be much sketchier than they are now, and the truth is that over the centuries we have lost track of his descendants.'

'Which is why we're so curious to know how it came to be in your dad's possession,' said Mrs M. 'It could very well be that he is distantly related to Conté. Which could potentially make him . . .'

'Conté's heir,' said Peanut.

'We think White might have realised that, once he saw you with the pencil,' said Mrs M. 'And one thing's for sure. He will *not* want your dad getting hold of it. Just in case our suspicions are correct.'

'Too right!' said Mr M. 'If your dad *is* Conté's heir, and the legends are to be believed, his wielding of Pencil Number One could undo all of White's efforts to destroy Chroma in one fell swoop!'

'MRS MARKMAKER! MR MARKMAKER!' A heavily muscled man, with long blond hair, wearing a Viking helmet and a huge spiky shoulder guard, suddenly burst into the Map Room. 'THE PRIMARY IS ON THE MOVE!'

'Oh! Right!' said Mr M. 'Er, thank you, Agent Odin the Stormbreaker. This is it! Quick! Let's go, Millicent. Peanut, Rockwell, Little-Bit, sit tight. We will be back as soon as we can. Whatever you do, don't leave the Bunker! We need to keep you safe. Doodle?' He looked at the dog still sitting on Little-Bit's lap. 'You're in charge, OK?' Doodle woofed his acknowledgement and wagged his tail.

'See you soon, dears,' said Mrs M, standing up and following her husband as he hurried out of the room. 'So sorry about this. Urgent Resistance business!'

Once the sound of footsteps running up the stairs had died down, Peanut spoke to the others. 'Are you guys thinking what I'm thinking?'

'That depends,' said Rockwell. 'Are you thinking of staying exactly where we are, having another cup of tea and maybe playing a nice game of I-Spy?'

'No,' said Peanut as she hid her sports bag under the table. 'I'm thinking that we follow Mr and Mrs M. I want to see what's going on. The Resistance might need our help.'

'In that case, I'm not thinking what you're thinking,' said Rockwell. 'You heard what they said, it's not safe for us out there.'

'Rocky, don't be such a baby,' said a gleeful Little-Bit. 'Where's your sense of adventure?'

19
Sketchwood

eanut, Rockwell and Little-Bit spent the next few
hours following the small band of Resistance
agents, which included the Markmakers, at a safe
distance, as they, in turn, followed a platoon of RAZERs, Mr
White and Alan. Doodle, who had decided to join in with the
children's mischief, led the way, following the Markmakers'
scent through the familiar charcoal forests and snow-covered
plains of the North Draw. After a couple of hours, they
passed the pink and blue Czech hedgehogs and the straggly
remains of the bright-blue, netted dome that surrounded the
entrance to the now abandoned bunker that had been the first
Resistance headquarters. Peanut felt a flash of anger. It was
here that Mr White had first got his hands on Little Tail.

Eventually, the convoy arrived at the forested area known as Sketchwood, and started to wind its way through the dusty black trees. Suddenly Doodle sat down and cocked his head to one side.

'They've stopped,' said Peanut looking straight ahead. 'Quick! Over there!'

All four of them hid behind a large charcoal tree trunk and peered around the side of it. It was hard to see exactly what was going on, but it looked as if the Markmaker group was hiding in a small copse about a hundred metres ahead of them.

Suddenly there was an explosion of activity. One member of the group sprang from the copse and started running at full speed towards Peanut and the gang. It was Agent Odin the Stormbreaker! Three RAZERs were in hot pursuit, gliding at a frightening speed across the snow. They caught up with the fleeing Resistance agent within seconds, and wasted no time in capturing him. Once he was bound, they picked him up and started carrying him, at speed, straight towards

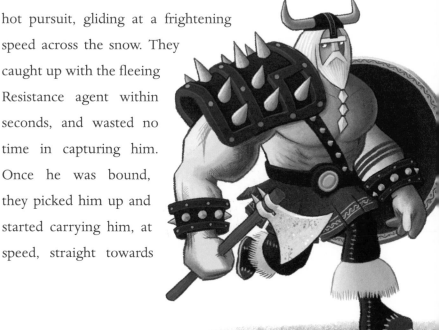

the tree that Peanut, Rockwell, Little-Bit and Doodle were hiding behind.

'Hurry! Get under this!' shouted Peanut, who had quickly painted a huge white inky square on the floor with her new roller. She lifted up a corner, and all four of them dived underneath it and held their breath.

Seconds later, they heard the three RAZERs whoosh by. Half a minute after that, they heard some more distant whooshing. Peanut peeped out from under their inky eiderdown.

'It's the rest of the RAZERs! Alan is there too! I'd recognise that chump anywhere! *Ssshhh!* They're coming!' She pulled her head back under just in time.

WHOOSH! WHOOSH! WHOOSH! WHOOSH! WHOOSH! WHOOSH! WHOOSH! WHOOSH! WHOOSH! They sounded like Formula One cars zooming past the chequered flag.

A minute later she tentatively peeped out again. 'OK, I think they've gone. Oh! Hang on, here come the Markmakers!' She ducked back underneath.

As the Resistance agents hurried past, the children could hear a great deal of consternation within the group and lots of panicked conversation.

'What are we going to do?'

'They'll put him in the Spire for sure!'

'What was he thinking?'

'Poor Agent Odin the Stormbreaker!'

'Maybe we can catch up with them and rescue him!'

'But Malcolm, what about the portal?'

'Some things are more important.'

'Did the target go through?'

'Yes, I saw him dive into the hollow.'

'But it's the final one. We should have sent someone through so we know where it leads!'

'We can come back later.'

'It could be too late by then.'

Peanut and the gang waited until the voices had faded into the distance, and then emerged from under the white-ink blanket.

'Well, that was close,' said Rockwell. 'I spy, with my little eye, something beginning with LUCKY ESCAPE!'

'Lucky is definitely the word,' said Peanut, smiling. 'As in "How lucky are we that everyone has disappeared and left us here on our own when there's a perfectly good portal to another world just a couple of hundred metres away?"'

'Oh no, you're not thinking—'

'I certainly am,' said Peanut, nodding. 'You heard the Markmakers. Someone from the Resistance needs to go through. Well, here we are! Let's go and find that portal!'

20

Into the Woods

The four of them walked deeper into the woods. If they were worried that they might not be able to find the portal, they needn't have been. When they got there, its location was blindingly obvious.

After walking for a couple of minutes they came across a small clearing, in the middle of which was a large tree, drawn very roughly, like all the others, in charcoal. It was made up of jagged, short strokes and, to Peanut's eye at least, resembled an upside-down lightning bolt with arms. These 'arms' were pointing to a large hollow, in the dead centre of its trunk.

'OK, so that's not creepy at all,' said Rockwell. 'I've just had an amazing idea, and it mainly involves running away really, really fast?'

'Look at it!' said Little-Bit. 'It's actually begging us to go through. Come on.'

She walked over to the trunk and started to climb the lower part. Peanut followed, and, eventually, so did a nervous

Rockwell. Doodle stayed where he was. He seemed to know what Peanut was about to say.

'I'm sorry, boy, but you can't come with us. We don't want you crumbling away to dust on the other side now, do we?'

Doodle's tail drooped.

'Maybe you should go back to the Bunker and tell everyone how crazy Peanut is being,' said Rockwell, as he slowly made his way up the trunk towards the hollow. 'And if you could also let them know where they can find our dead bodies, that'd be great!'

'*Ssshh!*' said Peanut, putting an ear to the large opening in the trunk. 'Can you hear that?'

'What?' said Little-Bit, hoisting herself up to sit on the edge of the hollow.

'Voices.'

'Actually, I can,' said Rockwell.

'Me too,' whispered Little-Bit. 'And I think they're speaking French!'

Then the three friends slipped into the hollow, and went through the North Draw portal.

Part Two

...in which Peanut
travels the world

21
Salle 345

Maman, pourquoi ses bras sont-ils tombés? Quelqu'un a-t-il laissé tomber la statue alors qu'il l'apportait à la galerie, ou le sculpteur a-t-il simplement manqué de temps?'

The door was only open a crack but the child's voice was as clear as a bell. Peanut looked back at the others with her finger to her lips.

'*C'est très, très vieux, mon chéri.*' A different voice this time. Female. And belonging to an adult. '*Crois-moi, vieillir est une chose brutale. Cela nous concerne tous. Allez, on doit retrouver papa rue Saint-Honoré dans dix minutes.*'

'*Je peux la toucher?*' The child again. '*Elle a l'air lisse.*'

'I wonder what they're saying,' whispered Rockwell.

'The little boy is telling his mum that the statue looks

very smooth,' said Little-Bit. 'And that he wants to touch it.'

'Oh, but *of course* you speak French! Hang on, what statue?'

'Quiet, you two. They'll hear,' whispered Peanut.

'*NON! CHRISTOPHE! ARRÊTE ÇA! LA CORDE EST LÀ POUR UNE RAISON!*' The woman was shouting now.

Some footsteps approached rapidly.

'*Excusez-moi, madame,*' said an officious-sounding man, '*mais la galerie ferme maintenant. S'il vous plaît, permettez-moi de vous montrer la sortie.*'

There was the sound of a slight kerfuffle before three sets of footsteps faded into the distance.

'OK,' whispered Peanut. 'I think the coast is clear.'

She pushed open the heavy door and the three children squeezed through. They found themselves in a large, grand room, with high, vaulted ceilings and red marble walls. To their left and right, huge arched openings led to equally opulent arcades, and straight ahead a statue-filled hallway, lined with ornate columns, seemed to go on for miles. The children stepped over a small glass barrier and turned to look back to see where they'd emerged from.

The sculpture was magnificent. An elegant female figure, two metres tall and beautifully carved from white marble.

'Er, where are her arms? Are they on display somewhere else?' said Rockwell.

'Don't be such a philistine, Rockwell,' said Peanut. 'It's obviously very old. Anyway, everybody knows that there's great beauty in imperfection. I think she's absolutely stunning.'

The statue stood on a large black plinth, the front of which had opened up like a door. Peanut hopped back over the barrier and pushed it shut. To her amazement, any evidence of the portal's existence totally disappeared as the door closed, apart from some very faint hinges and a tiny handle which looked like they had been drawn with a pencil.

Suddenly they heard footsteps in the arcade to their right. Quick as a flash, they hid in a shadowy alcove underneath one of the arches at the side of the room.

A small figure, dressed entirely in white, came trotting

into the gallery carrying a portrait of an enigmatic young woman in both hands. The person then stood in front of the statue, right on the spot where Peanut, Rockwell and Little-Bit had been seconds earlier, his white fedora glowing in the early evening light.

'It's him,' whispered Rockwell. 'It's Mr White!'

'*Hmm*. I recognise that painting . . .' said Peanut under her breath.

Mr White looked to his left, and then his right, checking that the coast was clear before stepping over the barrier. He pulled open the small door in the plinth and dived through.

'He's gone back to Chroma!' said Little-Bit. 'Why would he—'

Peanut put her hand over her sister's mouth.

A few seconds later, Mr White came back out of the portal, but he was no longer carrying the painting. He stood up, dusted himself down and pulled something yellow from his inside jacket pocket.

'Little Tail,' gasped Peanut.

He then closed the small door and rubbed at its four edges with the eraser end of the pencil. When he had finished, he blew the rubbings from the plinth's surface, stepped back over the barrier and proceeded to stroll nonchalantly away from the sculpture.

Just then, a security guard appeared at the far end of the hallway and approached Mr White.

'*Excusez-moi, monsieur,*' he said, '*mais la galerie est maintenant fermée. Veuillez vous diriger vers la sortie.*'

'*Bien sûr,*' said Mr White, his high voice echoing through the halls.

The children watched in silence as he casually walked down the corridor, before turning left and following a sign marked '*Sortie*'.

They waited for the security guard to turn the corner before emerging from their hiding place and following Mr White down a flight of stairs and into a huge subterranean atrium with a glass pyramid roof made up of hundreds of diamond-shaped panels.

'Ah! We're in the Louvre!' said Peanut, recognising the iconic glass structure. 'It's one of the biggest museums in the world and— *Wait . . . !* OMG! That painting Mr White was carrying! I knew I recognised it. HE'S STOLEN THE *MONA LISA!*'

'Well, I'm sure that's really terrible and everything,' said Rockwell, 'but I'm more worried about the fact that, because Mr White has rubbed out the portal, WE'RE TOTALLY TRAPPED HERE! Wherever *here* is.'

'Ooh, we're in Paris,' said Little-Bit, beaming. 'I've always wanted to go to Paris.'

'Paris. Right. Well, I don't see what you're looking so happy about,' said Rockwell. 'What are we going to do about being completely stranded in a foreign country without any money or passports or food?'

'*Shhh*, Rockwell! There he is,' said Peanut, pointing towards a spiral staircase at the far end of the hall. They watched as Mr White got to the top, went through a doorway in the pyramid's walls and sauntered out into the Parisian evening.

22
Leaving the Louvre

Keeping a safe distance, the children followed Mr White's route exactly, leaving the pyramid and walking into a large, paved courtyard, surrounded on three sides by imposing limestone pavilions.

Suddenly, an ear-splitting alarm began to sound, making them all jump. The high-pitched siren seemed to be coming from everywhere.

'WHAT'S GOING ON?' shouted Little-Bit.

'MY GUESS,' said Peanut, covering her ears, 'IS THAT THE WORLD'S MOST FAMOUS PAINTING HAS JUST CRUMBLED AWAY INTO DUST. OR AT LEAST WHAT THEY *THINK* IS THE WORLD'S MOST FAMOUS PAINTING HAS JUST CRUMBLED AWAY INTO DUST.'

A vast number of police officers started to spill out from the many doorways and colonnades in the pavilions lining the courtyard, all of them running at top speed towards the pyramid.

'*Sacrebleu!*' shouted one gendarme as he raced past the gang. '*Apparement, la* Joconde *vient de se désintégrer!*'

Meanwhile, fifty metres ahead of the children, the bright figure of Mr White was strolling in the opposite direction to the running policemen. Peanut watched as he disappeared through a large archway.

'COME ON! WE MUSTN'T LOSE HIM,' she shouted over the alarm.

The children scampered across the courtyard, through the archway and into another square. This one was much smaller, with a large fountain in the middle and four exits, one on each side.

'Which way did he go?'

'There!' said Rockwell, pointing to their right. This exit led straight out on to a wide road running parallel with a river.

'That must be the Seine,' said Little-Bit, proudly displaying her geographical knowledge.

'And look, there he is!'

Mr White was ambling across a bridge directly in front of them, straight towards a large, domed building on the opposite bank. The children followed, making sure to keep far enough back to avoid being spotted.

'So,' said Peanut, to herself as much as anyone, 'the sculpture on the plinth we came out of must have been the *Venus de Milo*. I can't believe I didn't recognise it! A year at St Hubert's and my artistic knowledge is already fading away . . .'

'Seriously though, how are we going to get back to Chroma?' said Rockwell. 'Or better still, home?'

'Listen. Do you remember when Mrs M said that White had been spotted back in the Spire an hour after going through the other portals around Chroma?'

Rockwell nodded.

'And we figured he must be making new portals with Little Tail each time to get back?'

He nodded again.

'Well, my guess is that he's going to make another one any minute now and nip through. So we just have to follow him.'

'Simple as that, is it?' said Rockwell sarcastically.

It was deep into the evening now. The sun had almost set and Paris was beginning to twinkle. As they walked across the bridge, they could see the Eiffel Tower to their right, rising majestically above the boulevards. It was lit up like a Christmas tree, shimmering and golden against the purple sky.

At the end of the bridge, Mr White crossed the road and turned left in front of the domed building. He then walked for a few hundred metres along the river's south

bank before turning right into the bustling streets of the Latin Quarter.

'We need to get a bit closer to him,' said Peanut, breaking into a jog. 'We don't want to lose him among the crowds.'

White picked up his pace slightly as he passed the boutiques and gift shops of Rue Dauphine and then negotiated the rows of parked bicycles and throngs of revellers outside the cocktail bars of Rue André Mazet. Once they'd crossed

into the narrow, pedestrianised Cour du Commerce Saint-André, the children found it a lot tougher to keep an eye on their quarry, as he weaved between the indecisive tourists and the turbo-charged waiters serving diners their al fresco meals.

'It smells so nice,' said Rockwell. 'Anyone else hungry?'

'Keep focused, Rockwell,' said Peanut. 'If we lose him, we are properly stuck.'

When they eventually emerged, blinking, on to the wide and brightly lit Boulevard Saint-Germain, they were relieved to see Mr White on the opposite side of the road. They still had him in their sights!

'Thank goodness he dresses to match his name,' said Little-Bit. 'Imagine how hard it'd be to spot him if he was called Mr Grey!'

He then made a left turn by a large corner cafe with a red awning, and walked south down Rue de l'Odéon. It was a long, straight road lined with clothes shops, all of which had closed for the day, so it was much quieter than the other streets. About halfway along, the gang ducked down behind a clumsily parked scooter and watched as Mr White slowed his pace.

'Is he going to that theatre?' whispered Rockwell.

He did appear to be approaching the grandiose, Roman-style building at the end of the street, but then, before he got there, he stopped and bent down.

'This feels strange,' said Peanut. 'What's he up to?'

'Is he tying his shoelace?' said Little-Bit.

'No, I don't think so.'

From his crouching position, Mr White placed both hands flat on the ground and started moving them quickly from side to side.

'What on earth is he doing?' said Rockwell.

'I . . . I think he's trying to lift something up,' replied Peanut.

Sure enough, with a sudden, sharp movement, Mr White stood up. He was holding something heavy-looking, rectangular and flat in his hands which he then put straight back down. From where they were, it looked to the children as if he'd grabbed part of the pavement and moved it to one side. He then dusted himself down, looked left and right, and . . . disappeared.

'Whoa!' said Rockwell. 'Did you see that? He just . . . dematerialised!'

'Quick! Let's go and have a look,' said Peanut.

The children ran to the corner of the road where Mr White had been standing. There was no sign of him.

'OK, this is freaking me out,' said Rockwell. 'How can someone just vanish into thin air?'

'He didn't vanish into the air,' said Little-Bit, pointing towards a large, slightly ajar manhole cover on the pavement. 'He vanished into the ground.'

23
The Catacombs

Between the two of them, Peanut and Rockwell managed to slide the heavy manhole cover to one side, revealing a deep, dark shaft and releasing a strong smell of damp into the warm night air.

'I'll go first,' said Peanut, turning around and carefully placing her foot on the first of the cast-iron rungs welded to the shaft's wall.

'Oh, so we're climbing into drains now, are we?' said Rockwell, as Peanut slowly descended into the void.

'You're not scared, are you?' she said, smiling as she looked up out of the hole.

'Scared? Yeah, right!' said Rockwell, swallowing hard. 'If anything, I'm looking forward to it.'

After a wobbly and considerably longer than expected descent, the three of them arrived at the bottom of the ladder, jumped the short distance from the final rung and landed with a splash.

'*UGH!* It's wet!' shrieked Rockwell.

'*Ssssh!*' said Peanut. 'We don't want Mr White to hear us.'

They were standing in a small, circular brickwork chamber with a very low ceiling, a slow, repetitive dripping noise ramping up the creepiness factor nicely. The dim light coming through the manhole high above their heads was just bright enough for them to be able to see five exits evenly distributed around the chamber's walls.

'OK, Sherlock, which way do we go now?' said Rockwell, who, being so tall, was having to stand with a slight bend in his knees.

'I'm not sure,' said Peanut. 'Maybe I should try drawing a torch or something.'

'We're not in Chroma now. You can't draw stuff that becomes real here. Not without Little Tail.'

'Good point.' Peanut was annoyed with herself for forgetting. 'OK, anyone have any ideas?'

'Well, speaking of torches,' said Little-Bit, staring at a large iron bracket bolted to the wet brick wall, 'I think there used to be one here.'

'Really? What, like, one of those flaming-stick things that

you see in old Robin Hood films?' asked Rockwell.

'Exactly like one of those,' she replied. 'And what's more, I'd say it's only been removed very recently.'

'Oh, come on, we might have gone through a couple of portals, but we haven't travelled five hundred years back in time!'

Little-Bit started to slowly pace around the room, sniffing the air.

'Er, so you're some sort of bloodhound now, are you?' said Rockwell.

Suddenly, the little girl stopped in front of one of the passageway entrances. 'He went this way!' she said confidently, before disappearing down it.

Rockwell and Peanut looked at each other, shrugged, and then followed her into the darkness.

24
'Arrêtez!'

'B, why are you so sure that Mr White went this way?' asked Peanut as they made their way along the dark, dank passageway.

'It's quite simple,' said Little-Bit. 'I'm just following the smell of sulphur dioxide.'

'Ooh, hang on! I know this one!' said Rockwell enthusiastically. 'Sulphur dioxide: the smell-making compound that's released when you strike a match. I remember that from Mrs Bloyce's chemistry class.'

'That's right,' said Little-Bit. 'It's the same smell given off by those flaming-stick things that you see in old Robin Hood films. So we literally have to follow our noses.'

'Guys,' whispered Rockwell after half an hour of sniffing their way through the tunnels. 'Has anybody stopped to think about the craziness of what we're doing? I mean, what happens if we don't find him? We're literally running around a weird maze of dark, spooky tunnels underneath Paris, and let's face it, we're totally lost.'

'We're not lost. And we *will* find him,' insisted Peanut. 'I know it.'

'Come to think of it, what happens if we *do* find him?' said Rockwell. 'Also, shouldn't we have been laying some kind of safety trail. You know, like Hansel and Gretel?'

'Rockwell, stop talking and start sniffing,' said Peanut sharply, although she did think that the trail idea was a good one.

'Wait! Did you see that?' said Little-Bit suddenly. 'Back there.'

'What? *OUCH!*' said Rockwell, looking over his shoulder and banging his forehead on the ceiling.

'I saw it too . . . A light,' said Peanut.

'*HÉ! ARRÊTEZ-VOUS!*' The officious voice was clear and alarmingly loud as it echoed up the passageway. It was closely followed by footsteps and a fast-moving, bouncing yellow beam of light that appeared around a corner twenty metres behind them.

'Run!' shouted Peanut.

'Where to?' yelled Rockwell, his escalating panic barely concealed beneath the surface.

'Just . . . go forwards!' she replied.

The three children dashed blindly through the catacombs, the sound of their pursuer's footsteps ringing in their ears. Their eyes had only partially adjusted to the darkness – they couldn't see more than a couple of metres ahead – so all three had their arms stretched out in front of them like zombies, hands flexed in anticipation of any unexpected dead ends.

'This way!' shouted Peanut. 'I can see a light at the end of the tunnel!'

'I sincerely hope you're speaking literally and not metaphorically!' said Rockwell.

Sure enough, there was a soft, golden glow filling the

tunnel up ahead. As she got closer, Peanut realised that it was coming from a vertical shaft, similar to the one they had climbed down to get into the catacombs in the first place. They skidded to a halt in the pool of light and frantically started to climb the iron rungs on the wall, Little-Bit first, then Peanut, and then, finally, Rockwell.

'*POLICE! ARRÊTEZ-VOUS! VENEZ-ICI!*' shouted the man chasing them, sounding very close now. He arrived at the bottom of the ladder as Rockwell reached the halfway point, then threw his torch to the floor and started to climb up after the children with impressive agility.

'HURRY UP!' screamed Rockwell to his friends. 'OH NO! HE'S GOT HOLD OF MY SHOE!'

'*JE TE TIENS MAINTENANT!*' said the policemen, his hand clasped to Rockwell's trainer.

'GET OFF ME!' shouted the boy, thrashing his leg around wildly while trying to maintain a grip on the rung. Rockwell felt the shoe slowly slipping from his foot, and with one last frantic kick it came off completely. He looked down to see the man fall from the ladder, a police cap flying from his head and Rockwell's favourite trainer in his hand.

25

Le Cimetière du Montparnasse

'Quick, Rockwell! Over here,' hissed Peanut, as her friend pulled himself clear of the manhole. He ran over to join the sisters, who were hiding behind a small, stone building hidden among trees.

'D-did you see that?' he stammered. 'He got my trainer!'

'Be quiet!' snapped Peanut. 'He's coming.'

Seconds later, they saw a dishevelled young gendarme with a black beard emerge from the opening, his police cap in one hand and Rockwell's shoe in the other. He dusted himself down and looked around, before running off in the opposite direction.

Peanut exhaled. 'That was close.'

'It was so FUN!' said Little-Bit. 'Can we do it again?'

'Er, I'd rather not! I'd like to retain at least one item of footwear, thank you very much. Now I know how Cinderella felt!' said Rockwell. He looked around. 'Right, so where are we now?'

The children were surrounded by avenues of stone buildings and monuments stretching away in all directions.

'Wow. These houses are all very small,' said Little-Bit.

'That's cos they're not houses,' said Peanut. 'They're tombs.'

'TOMBS?' said Rockwell, backing away from the stone wall that they were leaning on.

'Yes,' said Peanut. 'Look at what's on top of them all.'

Sure enough, the vast majority were topped with stone crosses or statues of angels, and many of the structures were far too low to house a person. At least, an upright person. Also, they all had names and dates carved into their walls, and were surrounded by freshly cut flowers.

'An entire city made of gravestones,' whispered Rockwell.

'It's actually le Cimetière du Montparnasse,' said Little-Bit, as she picked up a discarded leaflet from the ground and waved it at the others. 'Which means the Montparnasse Cemetery. Look, here's a little map.'

Peanut took the leaflet and opened it. Sure enough, it

featured a detailed, illustrated plan of the entire cemetery with a long list of names, in alphabetical order, on the right-hand side.

'Are those some of the people buried here then?' said Rockwell.

'Looks like it,' replied Peanut. 'The famous ones, I guess.'

'De Beauvoir, Beckett, Chirac, Conté, Gainsbourg, Man Ray, Sartre, Seurat . . .' Rockwell shook his head. 'Never heard of any of them.'

'Er, are you sure about that?' said Peanut.

'Yes!' said Rockwell, indignantly. 'De Beauvoir . . . De Beau-who? Beckett . . . nope. Chirac . . . sorry. Conté . . . no idea. Gainsbourg . . . not a clue. OH!' He paused. 'WAIT! CONTÉ? Is that *our* Conté? You know, the pencil bloke?'

'It must be!' said Peanut excitedly. 'It's too much of a coincidence otherwise!'

'Er, guys. I've found something else,' said Little-Bit. She was standing by a large wooden stick lying in the middle of the path. It had what looked like an old rag wrapped around the end of it which, strangely, was smoking. She picked it up (by the non-smoking end) and sniffed. 'Sulphur! This is the torch we were following through the tunnels. Mr White must have come up the same ladder we did. Which means . . .'

'Which means, he's here in the graveyard too,' said Peanut. 'But where? And why would he come *here*?'

A smile started to appear on Rockwell's face. 'You know what, guys? I think I know the answers to both of those questions.'

26
Conté's Grave

The children walked silently through the cemetery.

'If your theory is right, Rockwell, Mr White will be heading to Conté's grave,' said Peanut. 'So we need to find it quickly. Which way, Little-Bit?'

Little-Bit had been put in charge of map-reading and was leading them along the wide paths that served as 'streets'.

'If we carry on down here, turn left at the end, go past Serge Gainsbourg and Samuel Beckett, and then turn right on to that proper road bit, Conté should be somewhere on our left,' said Little-Bit confidently.

'OK. But we need to watch out for Mr White,' said a worried Rockwell. 'We don't want him to notice that we're following him.'

'I don't think he's spotted us yet,' said Peanut. 'Anyway, he's so focused on getting back to Chroma, he's probably not thinking about anything else.'

Five minutes later, they arrived at sector twenty-five, the area in which, according to the map, Conté's grave was to be found. The headstones and tombs were packed very tightly together, with every last bit of space being utilised. It was obviously a very popular place among dead Parisians.

'Right, Rockwell, you start checking the names over there,' said Peanut, pointing to the left, 'and LB, you take the right-hand side. I'll concentrate on the middle.'

Another five minutes passed before Little-Bit gleefully shouted, 'Found it!'

It was a fairly unremarkable memorial compared to some of those surrounding it. It comprised of a large, vertical headstone that sat at the end of a shallow, roof-shaped ledger, which Peanut thought reminiscent of an upturned book. On the headstone, a wreath containing a neat 'NJC' logo had been carved above the words '*CI-GÎT NICOLAS JACQUES CONTÉ*' and the dates of his birth and death. Two inverted torches (that bore distinct likenesses to pencils) featured in relief to the left and to the right of the inscription.

'What does *CI-GÎT* mean?' said Rockwell.

'*Here lies*,' replied Little-Bit. 'It says he was fifty when he died. Younger than Gran. That's very sad.'

Peanut and Rockwell, meanwhile, were examining the grave carefully.

'Any sign?' asked Rockwell.

'No evidence of a portal yet,' she said, walking around the headstone. 'There's nothing like those pencil hinges we saw on the *Venus de Milo's* plinth. There must be something here somewhere though . . . *A-HA!*'

'What?' said Little-Bit and Rockwell at the same time.

'Look,' said Peanut, pointing to the back of the headstone. 'Can you see?'

'Where?' asked Rockwell, squinting.

'A tiny door handle, drawn with a pencil. A very special pencil, I'll bet! I'd recognise that graphite anywhere.'

Sure enough, there was a very small doorknob drawn near the right edge. The shade of grey was exactly the same colour as the granite, so it was practically invisible.

'So Mr White *was* here!' said Little-Bit. 'You were right, Rocky!'

'Well? What are you waiting for?' said Rockwell. 'Let's get this over with.'

Peanut turned the knob, and the three of them heard the faint clicking sound of a latch releasing. She pulled, and, as if by magic, a door the full width of the stone began to open.

'Here we go again,' said Peanut, swallowing hard. 'Heaven knows where we'll end up this time.'

27
The Room with the Doors

They emerged into a dimly lit, circular room with a very high ceiling that rose in a tall, thin cone shape to a central peak fifteen metres above their heads.

'Are we in a giant wigwam?' said Rockwell.

'If we are, it's a very high-tech one,' said Peanut, walking over to the massive console opposite the door they'd come through. The three-metre-wide desk resembled the ones she'd seen in photographs of famous rock stars in their recording studios. It was jam-packed with switches, levers, dials, sliders, flashing diodes, small LCD displays and illuminated buttons. And the vast majority of the buttons were glowing green, casting an eerie light across the faces of the children.

'Ooh, it's like the flight deck of the Millennium Falcon,' said Rockwell, smiling. 'I've always wanted to be a starpilot.' He then proceeded to press as many of the green buttons as he could, delighting in the fact that they turned red as he did so.

'Careful, flyboy,' said Peanut. 'We don't want to get captured by Darth Vader. So, what's with the screens?'

On the wall behind the console was a grid of video monitors, each one displaying grainy, black-and-white security-camera footage of streets, fields, buildings and bridges. Each one had letters printed just above it.

'*Hmmm.* ND, ID, S, LD, VF, DB, W . . .' said Little-Bit as she read. 'Ah, got it! They're the districts of Chroma! North Draw, Ink District, Strip, Light District, Vincent Fields, Die Brücke, Warholia . . .'

'Of course!' said Peanut. 'We must be back in the Illustrated City. And this must be some sort of . . . observation room?'

'Wait a second,' said Little-Bit, looking up at the high, pointed ceiling. 'You don't think we're in a room right at the top of—'

'The Spire!' shouted Peanut. 'Yes! I think we might be!'

'Well, it would certainly make sense for Mr White to draw a portal that would lead straight back to his headquarters,' replied Little-Bit.

'So what are those, then?' said Rockwell, looking at the wall behind them.

Surrounding the open portal that they'd just stepped through were eleven other doors, crudely drawn in pencil and, again, with different initials written above each one.

'I would guess they are other portals that he's drawn,'

said Peanut. 'Maybe he always draws a new one to travel home through. And they all lead back here.'

'His own private collection of gateways between the worlds, that nobody else knows about . . .' whispered Little-Bit.

Rockwell, who had walked around the console and was standing a few metres to the girls' left, was looking down

at the floor. 'What's this trapdoor?'

Sure enough, there was a large, wooden hatch, set into the middle of one of the concrete flagstones.

'Only one way to find out,' said Peanut, running to join him. 'Let's open it.'

The two of them pulled the iron handle as hard as they could and lifted one of the doors.

'Is that . . . a swimming pool?' said Peanut, looking inside.

'Yes,' replied Rockwell. 'And it looks as if it's full of rainbow-coloured water.'

She nodded. 'It does. White must have been stealing water from the Rainbow Lake! What on earth is he up to?'

'Er, Peanut. You might want to come over here.' Little-Bit was now on the far side of the room, staring at a collection of large objects propped up against the curved wall.

'Is that . . . ?'

'The *Mona Lisa*,' said Little-Bit. 'Yes. And look, there's a painting that looks like the sky in Vincent Fields. And here's a really expensive-looking golden trophy of some sort.'

'Er, that's the Jinou Yonggu Cup! I drew a picture of it when I was at Melody High. It's the priceless work of art from China that disintegrated a few weeks ago! And these are the other "missing" pieces from the galleries around the world!' cried Peanut. 'The ones that supposedly turned to dust. That's the Dali self-portrait, that sculpture is the Henry Moore, and unless I'm mistaken, this one –' she folded back the end of a large roll of canvas, at least three and a half metres tall, that was propped up against the wall – 'is *Guernica* by Picasso. The one that disappeared this morning!'

'So we have proof!' said Little-Bit. 'Mr White *is* stealing them and replacing them with fakes!'

'Guys. Forget about priceless works of art,' said Rockwell. 'I've just found something much more valuable.'

The two girls rushed back to the console. And there, sitting snugly in a small groove at the far end of the desk, was an old yellow pencil.

28
'NYC'

ittle Tail!' yelled Peanut. She grabbed the pencil and held it flat in the palms of both hands. Once again, she was surprised at how heavy it was. 'Oh, how I've missed you,' she said.

'*Sssh!*' said Rockwell. 'I think someone's coming.'

Sure enough, they heard footsteps and muffled voices just outside the door next to the monitors. The children could just about make out what was being said.

'Yes, sir. I'll make sure it's taken care of,' said the first voice.

'You do that! And try not to mess it up this time,' said the second, in a much higher tone.

'Oh no,' whispered Peanut 'I think that might be . . .'

The door swung open and in walked two very different, but very familiar-looking figures. The first, dressed in a black suit, was tall and muscular, with huge shoulders, a neck as wide as his head and a pale face spattered with orange freckles. The second was much shorter, and wore a suit so white that it was positively luminous. On top of his head, angled down to cover his eyes, was an equally bright fedora hat.

'. . . Mr White!' said Rockwell. 'And Alan!'

The two newcomers to the room immediately stopped moving and looked, wide-eyed and open-mouthed, at the children. That tiny pause was just about long enough for

Peanut to act. She thrust Little Tail into the empty slot on her bandolier, grabbed hold of Little-Bit's hand and Rockwell's rucksack, and dragged them both towards the rear wall. She quickly scanned the illustrated doors in front of her, made a decision, and kicked open the one marked 'NYC'.

'GO! GO! GO!' she bellowed, practically throwing her sister and her best friend through the portal. As she dived after them, she heard the higher voice cry out from behind her.

'NOOOOOOOOOOOOOOOOOOOOOOO!'

Blood, Stone & Partners, New York

The three of them came flying out of the cupboard and landed in a heap on the wooden floor, alongside a beige raincoat and two umbrellas that they appeared to have collected en route.

'OMG,' gasped Rockwell as he tried to catch his breath. 'Where are we now? What shall we do?'

Peanut looked around, mindful of the fact that Mr White and Alan, his rather large henchman, would be following them through the portal VERY soon. They were in an office, a bit like her mum's back in London, with wood-panelled walls, a huge mahogany desk and a giant iron chandelier hanging

from the ceiling. Apparently, they had entered via a small coat cupboard to the right of the desk.

She scrambled to her feet. At the end of the room was a door with a frosted-glass panel filling the top half. Peanut could just about make out the words 'Blood, Stone & Partners, New York' printed on the other side of the glass.

'THAT WAY!'

The three of them ran out of the room as quickly as they could, and found themselves in a long corridor, lined with lots of identical semi-glazed doors. 'IN THERE!' shouted Peanut, pointing to the one door that didn't have a glass panel and was slightly ajar. They piled inside and pulled it shut.

The whole operation took about three seconds.

30
Inside the Janitor's Closet

The darkness was the can't-see-your-own-hand-in-front-of-your-face kind. Three more seconds passed before Peanut, Rockwell and Little-Bit heard a door in the corridor open and some fast-moving footsteps.

'I'M HOLDING YOU PERSONALLY RESPONSIBLE FOR THIS, ALAN.'

It was Mr White. He was shouting, so his already shrill voice was a couple of octaves higher than usual.

'I'm s-s-sorry, sir. B-but it wasn't actually me that left the p-pencil on the—'

'THIS IS NO TIME FOR NITPICKING!' shrieked Mr White. 'DO YOU KNOW HOW IMPORTANT THAT PENCIL IS? THE WHOLE PLAN DEPENDS ON MY HAVING IT! I STILL HAVE ONE MORE OF THE ORIGINAL PORTALS TO RUB OUT. GAH! WE'RE SO CLOSE TO PUTTING A STOP TO THIS WHOLE CHROMA THING ONCE AND FOR ALL!'

'Yes, sir. I realise—'

'AND DO YOU KNOW HOW DANGEROUS THAT PENCIL COULD BE TO US IN THE WRONG HANDS? EVERYTHING WE ARE WORKING TOWARDS IS AT RISK!'

'Y-yes, sir. Of c-course, sir. I just—'

'HOW ON EARTH DID THEY GET INTO MISSION CONTROL ANYWAY?'

'Th-they must have followed you, sir. I noticed when we entered the room that the Paris portal was open.'

'NONSENSE!' shrieked Mr White. 'I RUBBED IT OUT AS USUAL, JUST AFTER I THREW THE PAINTING BACK THROUGH THE DOOR.'

'Not that portal, sir. The n-new one.'

'OH! YES, I KNEW THAT!' bellowed White. 'I WAS JUST CHECKING THAT YOU WERE PAYING ATTENTION. SO THEY MUST HAVE FOLLOWED ME THROUGH THE ORIGINAL PORTAL IN THE NORTH DRAW AND THEN ACROSS PARIS TO CONTÉS ...

The voices trailed off as Mr White and Alan continued down the corridor.

'So the Markmakers were right,' whispered Peanut. 'Thank goodness you spotted the pencil, Rockwell. Now we at least have a chance of stopping him. Great job!'

Rockwell felt his cheeks redden. Just as he was thinking how glad he was that the girls couldn't see him blush, light filled the room. He looked over at Peanut, who was holding a slightly wonky-looking pencil drawing of a lightbulb.

'Yeah, it's not great, is it?' she said, smiling. 'That's what happens when you draw in the dark. Right, let's get out of here before Mr White and Alan come back, shall we?'

'Before we go, will you do me a favour?' said Rockwell. 'Would you draw me another shoe?'

31
The Elevator

Rockwell carefully slipped the rather fetching drawing of a trainer on to his foot.

'Just try not to touch it with your fingers,' said Peanut. 'That's what seems to initiate the crumbling process.' Right on cue, the illustrated lightbulb in her hand flickered as the drawing started to disintegrate. 'See? Right. Time to go.'

She opened the door a few centimetres and peeped through the crack. The corridor was empty.

'All clear,' she said, before leading the party

out of the janitor's closet. At the far end of the long hallway she could see three black doors, beautifully inlaid with a gold, art deco design. As they got closer, the children saw that above each one was a slowly rotating needle pointing to a series of numbers on a semi-circular panel. 'Lifts. Perfect!'

The elevators were situated at the mid-point of another corridor, perpendicular to the one they'd just walked down. Peanut pushed the '▼' button next to the door on the left, and watched as the needle began to move from its position pointing to number 3 around to the right.

'This must be a very tall building,' said Little-Bit. 'The numbers go up to a hundred and two.'

'Well don't worry about that, cos we're going down,' replied Peanut.

'Thank goodness for that,' said Rockwell, sounding relieved. 'I'm not a huge fan of heights.'

'THERE THEY ARE!'

The voice came from their right.

'GET THEM, YOU IDIOT!' shouted Mr White, as Alan,

at the far end of the corridor, broke into his rather lumbering version of a sprint.

Peanut glanced up at the dial. The arrow had stopped at number 24.

'Press the other buttons!' she yelled.

Rockwell and Little-Bit did as they were told and, luckily, a bell rang and the middle door immediately slid open.

'GET IN!' shouted Peanut, and, for the second time in less than two minutes the three of them dived through a door. To their right was a panel covered in numbered buttons. 'Quick! Press 1!'

Rockwell hit the one at the very top of the panel, and to their relief the doors started to close immediately.

'STOP THAT LIFT!'

Mr White's voice, increasing in volume with every word, accompanied the *thud-thud-thud* of Alan's rapidly approaching footsteps. The doors seemed to take an eternity to shut. The children watched helplessly as the opening shrank from fifty centimetres to thirty to ten to five. Just before the doors met in the middle, four large, freckle-covered fingers shot through and gripped the edge. Without thinking, Rockwell pulled off his new shoe and started repeatedly hitting Alan's hand with it.

'OW! THAT REALLY HURTS!' shrieked the henchman, before letting go, allowing the doors to slam shut.

Peanut and Little-Bit stared at Rockwell. He looked back at them, eyes wide with shock, while the shoe crumbled to dust in his hand.

'Oh well,' he said, as the fine, silvery grey powder ran through his fingers to the floor. 'Easy come, easy go.'

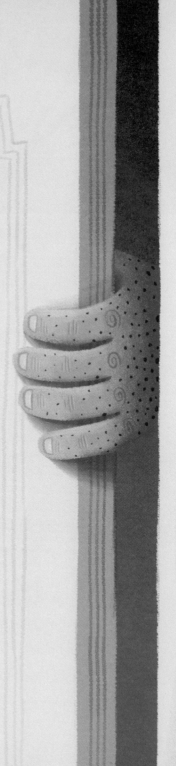

32
Going Up

'Rocky, why on earth did you press the top-floor button?' said Little-Bit.

'Look, I panicked,' replied the boy. 'I didn't exactly have time to consider my options. I just pressed anything!'

'Well, next time try to think it through.'

'Oh, I'm so sorry! Maybe I should have just let that big, massive ginger bloke open the door and catch us. Anyway, what "next time"? I'm not actually planning on making this a regular occurrence!'

'Quiet, you two,' snapped Peanut. 'I'm trying to concentrate.' She was kneeling,

furiously drawing three large sketches in mid-air with Little Tail. 'What floor are we on?'

'Seventy-four,' said Little-Bit. 'No, seventy-eight. Eighty! Eighty-three! And we're heading up to one hundred and two. It says "Observation Deck" next to it.'

Thirty seconds later, there was a *ding* sound, and the doors slid open.

'Right. This one's for you, LB, and this one's for you, Rockwell,' said Peanut, pointing to the drawings. 'Try not to touch them with your hands as you put them on.' Floating near the floor of the elevator were three drawings of what looked like rucksacks. The children all crouched down and reversed into them, awkwardly hooking their arms through the graphite shoulder straps. Once the drawings were safely on their backs, they turned left out of the elevator.

'Oh no,' said Peanut, looking at the floor-to-ceiling glass windows that surrounded them. 'It's not an open-air observation deck!'

'That's a good thing, isn't it?' said Rockwell. 'Much safer. After all, we don't want to go over the edge.'

'On the contrary,' said Peanut, looking around. 'Right! This way!'

They headed back past the lift, through a small door to their left and up a flight of stairs.

'Er, Peanut? What did you mean when you said "on the contrary"?' asked Rockwell nervously as they climbed.

'Oh, don't worry about it,' replied Peanut. 'Let's just get to the top of these stairs as quickly as we can, shall we?'

Suddenly they heard a familiar *ding* behind them, followed by the sound of lift doors opening.

'THERE THEY ARE! GET UP THOSE STAIRS, YOU BLOCKHEAD!' Mr White's dulcet tones signalled to the children that they had company.

As the children got to the top of the metal staircase, they heard the clanging sound of Alan's heavy footsteps at the bottom. As quickly as she could, Peanut pulled open the heavy steel door in front of them, which immediately flooded the dark stairwell with sunlight. Then the three of them ran out into the fresh air.

'WHOA!' shouted Rockwell, windmilling his arms backwards as he came to a sudden stop. 'We are *very* high up! And that barrier is *very* low down!'

The children looked out, past the waist-high concrete

wall that lined the narrow walkway surrounding the top of the building. The view was breathtaking. Thousands of tall, grey buildings, packed tightly together like concrete redwoods in an urban forest, stretched to the horizon. The city was bordered on each side by water, and punctuated by a large area of greenery in the centre. In any other circumstance, one that didn't involve them running for their lives, it would have been perfect Instagram fodder.

'I hate to say this, Peanut,' said Little-Bit, 'but I think we might be trapped.'

'WE'RE DEFINITELY TRAPPED!' echoed Rockwell loudly. 'OH NO, WHY ME?'

'Guys,' said Peanut calmly. 'Do you trust me?'

'WHAT?' shrieked Rockwell. 'NOW IS NOT THE TIME FOR POSITIVE REINFORCEMENT!'

'Do . . . you . . . trust . . . me?' repeated Peanut slowly.

'Of course we do!' said Little-Bit.

'Well, in that case promise me you'll do exactly as I tell you. Whatever that may be.'

'OK. I promise,' said Little-Bit.

'Rockwell?'

'YES! WHATEVER! I PROMISE!' said the near-hysterical boy.

At that moment, Alan and Mr White appeared in the doorway behind them.

'Well, well, well. If it isn't Miss *Pernilla* Jones,' sneered Mr

White. 'Fancy seeing you here. Having a nice little outing with your friends, are we?'

'It's *Peanut*, actually! And we know all about you, Mr White. That you're stealing the world's greatest works of art so that you have them all to yourself. It's quite the plan. And nothing could bring me more pleasure than scuppering it!'

'Ha!' said Mr White, holding on to his fedora to stop the wind blowing it from his head. 'I think that may be wishful thinking, young lady. I don't know if you've noticed, but you are currently standing one hundred and three floors above Manhattan with nowhere to go. I'm not sure you're in a position to be scuppering anything. Alan, shut that door, will you? We don't want our friends to leave the party early, do we?'

'Oh well done, genius,' said Peanut after Alan had closed the steel door with a loud click. 'There's no handle on the outside. We're all locked out now. Good luck getting back in.'

The smile disappeared from Mr White's face and he shot Alan a venomous look. He turned back to Peanut and glanced at her bandolier. 'Enough of this chit-chat. Give me back that pencil, little girl. If you hand it over without making a fuss, I might consider sparing you and the rest of the kindergarten class here.'

'Rockwell, Little-Bit,' said Peanut, looking at her companions. 'This is the part where you have to trust me.'

They both nodded.

Peanut climbed up on to the concrete barrier, and stood up gingerly as the wind whipped around her.

'What do you think you are doing?' said Mr White.

'I w-was about to s-say the same thing,' said Rockwell.

'Come on, you two,' said Peanut. 'Get up here. Remember what I said.'

Rockwell lifted Little-Bit on to the top of the wall before carefully climbing up himself. His knees were actually knocking together, like something out of a comic book.

'OK, this is what we are going to do,' whispered Peanut. 'When I count to three, we are going to step off the wall.'

'S-s-step off the wall?' repeated Rockwell.

'Yes. And when you do, I want you to *immediately* press the button that I have drawn on the right shoulder strap of your backpack.'

Little-Bit glanced down at the strap, and sure enough it featured a large round button right in the centre. She turned to Rockwell and put a hand on his arm. 'Look. I'm scared too, Rocky, but we have to trust Peanut. We promised.'

Rockwell looked at the little girl. 'You're right,' he said. 'We have to try.'

'It'll be all right, guys,' said Peanut seriously. 'As long as you press the button straight away. I can't emphasise enough how important it is that you do that.'

She took a deep breath. 'OK. One . . .'

'Right. Enough of this nonsense,' said Mr White. 'Joke's over, kiddiewinks. Time to get down from the ledge.'

'Two . . .'

'Alan, grab them!'

'THREE!' shouted Peanut, before the three children stepped out into the void.

33

We Have Lift Off

As they began to fall, Peanut, Rockwell and Little-Bit pressed their buttons simultaneously, and immediately the rockets at the base of their backpacks roared into action. Hot, powerful bursts of yellow and orange pastel dust shot vertically downwards from the jets, slowing the three children's descent and filling their bodies with a strange feeling of weightlessness.

'*YEEEEEE-HAAAAWWWWW!*' cried Little-Bit as she hovered in mid-air. 'JET-PACKS! THESE ARE THE BEST DRAWINGS YOU'VE EVER DONE, PEANUT!'

'MY TUMMY FEELS FUNNY,' said a rather green-looking Rockwell.

Peanut looked back up at the ledge they'd been standing

on only a moment before. They were, by now, a good ten metres below Mr White and Alan, who were both looking down in astonishment from the top of the building.

'OK! JUST TIP YOURSELF FORWARDS TO GO DOWN, LEAN LEFT TO TURN LEFT, AND RIGHT TO TURN RIGHT,' shouted Peanut as she began to descend in a smooth, zigzag pattern through the sky. 'FOLLOW ME!'

Little-Bit did as she was told, and slotted nicely into Peanut's slipstream, following her every turn like a duckling trailing her mother.

Meanwhile, Rockwell, who had now added a somewhat startled expression to his green-tinged face, tipped too far forwards and did a full somersault, before shooting straight up at about seventy miles an hour and disappearing into a cloud.

'ER, PEANUT!' shouted Little-Bit looking heavenward. 'I DON'T THINK ROCKY'S GOT THE HANG OF THIS.'

A few seconds later, a loud cry of

'WHOOOOOOOOOOOAAAAAA

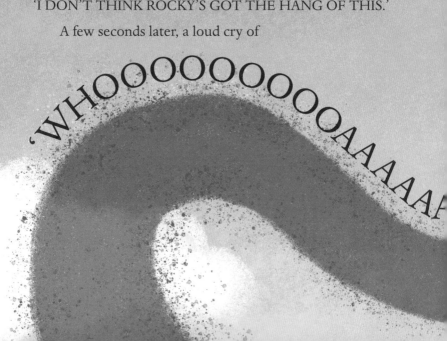

AAHHHHHH!

preceded Rockwell's re-entry. He came flying out of the cloud, thrashing around like he was riding a bucking bronco at the funfair. Following a series of inelegant, jerky movements, he managed to gain a semblance of control over his jet-pack and fall into line behind the other two.

They continued their long descent without further incident until they were about fifteen metres above the sidewalk, at which point all three pencil-drawn jet-packs slowly started to disintegrate. First, the rockets themselves began spluttering, then the shoulder straps started to crumble.

'I think it's because we had to press the buttons at the top,' said Peanut. 'Only a slight touch, but it started the process. Hang in there, guys. We're nearly down now.'

By the time they were a couple of metres from the ground, the straps had disappeared entirely, closely followed by the rest of the packs. Fortunately, their forward momentum meant that they could safely jump the last metre, and make a reasonably dignified, if speedy, running landing.

'Thank the Maker!' said Rockwell, as he knelt down and kissed the concrete. 'Never have I been so glad to be on the ground. Although,' he added, grabbing his shoeless foot, 'I think I've taken some skin off! Ouch!'

'Give me a second,' said Peanut, pulling Little Tail from her bandolier, 'and I'll draw you another shoe.'

As Peanut sketched, Little-Bit and Rockwell took a

moment to take in their surroundings. They were standing on a wide pavement next to a busy road, in front of the *very* grand entrance to the huge building they'd just visited. Despite being enveloped by a large plume of steam coming from a manhole cover in front of them, Little-Bit could just about make out the words embossed in gold on the art deco facade twenty metres above their heads.

'Peanut,' said Little-Bit. 'I think we've just jumped from the top of the Empire State Building.'

34
Times Square

'Ooh, I've always wanted to go to New York,' said Rockwell, whose face was slowly returning to its normal colour.

'Right. Put this on,' said Peanut, pointing to her drawing.

'Really?' he said, frowning.

'I think it suits you,' said Little-Bit.

A small crowd was starting to gather around them.

'You see that?' yelled a man holding some pizza and wearing a hi-vis vest. 'They came flying down through the steam and landed right here on the sidewalk. I almost dropped my slice!'

'I saw it too,' shouted a blonde woman in a pinstripe suit. 'Is this a stunt for a

TV show or something? Are we on *Conan*?'

'Yeah, what's poppin', kids?' said a young man whose camouflage trousers were just about covering his bottom. 'They was some crazy moves, yo!'

'I think we should make ourselves scarce before Mr White and Alan manage to open that steel door and get the next lift down,' said Peanut quietly to the others. 'More attention is the last thing we need. Let's disappear into the crowd.'

The three children ran around the corner and started to weave between the masses of people, doing their best to lose their newfound admirers amid the bustle of the city. As they walked past the luggage outlets, sports stores and souvenir shops, they looked up. The sheer height of the buildings around them was quietly blowing their minds.

'I feel as if we're in a film,' said a gawping Rockwell.

'I've never seen so many flags in my life,' said Little-Bit, looking up at the multitude of Star-Spangled Banners fluttering in the breeze.

The gang turned right, on to Broadway, passing a huge department store claiming to be the biggest in the world, and headed, like moths drawn to a flame, towards the distant neon glow of Times Square.

After a few minutes, they arrived at a large, incredibly busy pedestrianised area, surrounded on all sides by more unbelievably tall buildings. This time, however, they were

completely covered by a host of huge video screens, each one trying to shout more loudly than the next about the product they were advertising.

On a four-storey screen to their right, directly below a hamburger advertisment, a twenty-four-hour news channel

was playing. They appeared to be running a story about the recent disintegration of the *Mona Lisa*.

'Ooh, look!' shouted Little-Bit. 'There's the security guard we saw in the Louvre.' Sure enough, the man they had so recently watched asking Mr White to leave the gallery was standing next to the wall on which the *Mona Lisa* had been hanging, now looking forlornly at a pile of silvery grey dust on the floor.

'We need to get back,' said Peanut suddenly. 'The Resistance needs our help.' It was as if she had been woken from a dream. She pulled Little Tail from her bandolier. 'I'm going to draw a door.'

'Er, don't you think we should go somewhere a bit more . . . private?' said Rockwell, looking around at the busiest part of one of the world's busiest cities.

'Actually,' said Peanut, looking at the various buskers, mime artists and acrobats who were scattered across the square, 'I think this is the perfect place to do it.'

She started to draw. As usual, the graphite flowed smoothly from the pencil's tip, leaving a thick, dark line, perfectly suspended in mid-air, in its wake. Almost immediately, a crowd formed in a horseshoe shape around them. With each pencil stroke, the *'oohs'* and *'ahhs'* got louder. By the time Peanut had drawn the door's handle, they were applauding enthusiastically and throwing coins and dollar bills at Peanut's feet. Rockwell scooped up a handful of money and ran over to a food cart a few metres away. He came back two minutes later carrying three of the biggest hot dogs the girls had ever seen.

'Do you want one?' he said, just as Peanut was putting the finishing touches to the panelling on the door.

After adding the hinges while eating her hot dog, Peanut turned around and bowed deeply as the growing crowd whooped their appreciation, before turning back to face the door. She took a deep breath, grabbed the handle and opened it. More gasps from the crowd. She turned and bowed again, before grabbing Little-Bit's hand, and leading her through the open door.

Rockwell, standing in the crowd munching on his hot dog, happily joined in the applause. Then, suddenly remembering what was going on, he threw the food in the nearest bin, wiped the mustard from the corner of his mouth, and darted through the open door, pulling it shut behind him.

The cheers of the crowd could be heard across the dimensions.

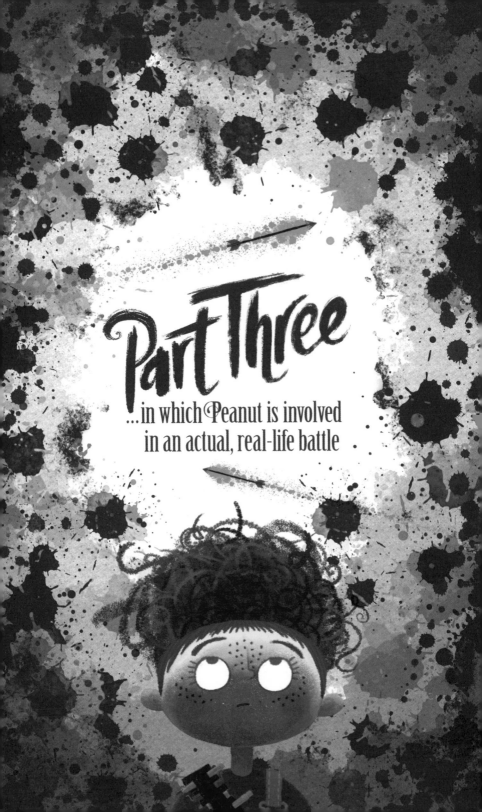

Part Three

...in which Peanut is involved
in an actual, real-life battle

35
Warholia

Rockwell shut the door on New York City, and turned around to find himself standing in a vast, slightly scruffy warehouse. Eight concrete columns held up the high ceiling, which was crawling with exposed, snake-like pipework, huge sheets of silver foil, and photographic spotlights hanging from the rafters. Peanut and Little-Bit were standing at the far end of the room admiring several large canvases that were leaning up against the wall. They all featured the same screen-printed picture of flowers, but each employed a different colourway.

'Hi, guys,' said Rockwell, walking up to them. 'Long time no see. I hate to ask again, but, er, where on God's green earth are we now?'

'Judging by these paintings, I'd say we're in Warholia,' replied Peanut.

Little-Bit nodded her agreement. 'The district named after the famous American pop artist Andy Warhol.'

'Peanut, why does your sister know literally everything in the world?' said Rockwell, turning away from the painting. 'It's really weird and, frankly, quite annoy—'

He froze mid-word, his mouth agape.

'What's wrong?' asked Peanut, turning to see what her friend was staring at.

On the other side of the warehouse, blocking the large floor-to-ceiling doorway, were seven tall, silver robots. They were totally still, floating about thirty centimetres above the floor and staring menacingly back at the children.

'P-P-Peanut,' stammered a terrified Rockwell, who was frozen to the spot, 'R-R-RAZERs!'

'OK, be calm,' said Peanut, reaching for Little Tail and looking around the room for possible exits. 'I-I'll think of something.'

Little-Bit, meanwhile, was looking at the RAZERs and frowning. She started walking towards them.

'LB, what are you doing? COME BACK HERE!' shouted Peanut.

'It's OK,' said Little-Bit, approaching the RAZER with the number 105 stencilled on to its torso and staring up at its face. 'Yes. Just as I thought . . .'

'Wh-wh-wh-what?' shouted Rockwell, who was slowly backing away. 'Wh-what's just as you thought?'

'They're not working. Look. Their eyes aren't lit up.'

She was right. Usually, the RAZERs' eyes glowed either red or green, but these ones were totally dark.

'It's like . . . they've been deactivated,' whispered Peanut, and she walked over and gently kicked the base of one with her boot. 'They're not getting any power. It's as if someone's turned them off. How strange. I wonder what's going on.'

Meanwhile, Rockwell had slowly made his way over to the warehouse door, careful to give the robots a wide berth. Something large and bright red had caught his eye just outside the doorway. 'What's this?' he said. 'It looks like . . . a giant can of Coke.'

Sure enough, an enormous soft-drink can, about five metres tall, was standing on the pavement. It was perfectly detailed, right down to the great big price sticker near the top, and a small dent carefully sculpted into the side to make it look like the can had, at some point, been dropped.

'Wow!' said Peanut. 'It's some kind of art installation. Isn't it magnificent!'

'Look,' said Little-Bit. 'There are more of them.'

It was true. A whole row of giant Coke cans lined the street. The effect was mesmerising.

'It feels like we've been shrunk and put on a supermarket shelf,' whispered Peanut.

The second-to-last can had been made to look like it had fallen over and spilt its contents on to the pavement.

It was so convincing that Peanut was surprised to see several children splashing around in the sticky spillage. But as they got closer, she realised that it was actually a paddling pool full of coloured water carefully made to look like a puddle of cola.

The opposite side of the street held even more wonder, its buildings resembling the items you would usually find in a shopping basket.

'Come on,' said Peanut. 'We have to get back to the Bunker and tell the Markmakers that we've got Little Tail back. Let's get going.'

'We've got a pretty long walk ahead of us,' said Little-Bit. 'Remember, the Bunker is in the northern part of the Green Valleys. Can't you paint us something that will make the journey quicker? Mr White will be back in Chroma soon. Well, once he's made his way down from the top of the Empire State Building and through the portal in the Blood, Stone & Partners office.'

'Yes, but remember that weird time thing: ten minutes in the real world is four hours in the illustrated world,' said Rockwell.

'LB's right, though,' said Peanut. 'Something to help us get there quicker would be good. Let's go back to the warehouse. I've got an idea.'

36
The Balloon

When the group got back to the warehouse, Peanut got to work. First, she pulled Little Tail from the bandolier and drew a large basket, big enough for the three children to stand in. She then painted a series of huge sausage-like shapes.

'You guys need to help me with these,' she said, placing her watercolours on the floor. 'Use any colours you like.'

Half an hour, and a lot of paint, later, it was ready.

The children stood back and admired their work.

'Wow,' said a smiling Rockwell, his face spattered with coloured paint flecks. 'I can't believe *we've* made this! I feel super-proud!'

'It's going to brighten up the whole sky,' said Little-Bit.

'Yes. That'll show Mr White that he's got a long way to go before he gets rid of all the colour in Chroma. Great work, team,' said Peanut. 'Right, Rockwell, first I need a bit of help with the physics, then let's drag it outside and get on our way.'

'Sure thing, boss. You just need to draw a burner, a couple of propane tanks and a parachute valve, and we're all set.'

As they drifted over Chroma in their hot-air balloon-animal, Peanut, Rockwell and Little-Bit looked down at the city below. Despite the sun being low in the evening sky, they could easily make out the quirky buildings of Warholia that they'd just seen from ground level, as well as skyscrapers made entirely of scouring pad and cereal boxes, a lipstick power station, and, randomly, a giant shuttlecock in the middle of a field.

As they crossed into the skies above Dali Point West, the landscape below them began to change dramatically. The industrial feel of Warholia was replaced by a sandy desert-like landscape. There were several lakes packed with enormous swans and surrounded by tall trees with ladders instead of trunks. Herds of strange-looking elephants wandered between enormous eggs, melting clocks and giant old-fashioned telephones, their legs so long and spindly that it looked like they were walking on stilts.

'Well, that's something you don't see every day,' said Rockwell.

'Look!' said Peanut. 'Can you see all those platoons of RAZERs? None of them are moving. It's like they've *all* been deactivated.'

'You don't think we did that, do you?' said Little-Bit.

'What do you mean?'

'Well, you know when we were in that room at the top of the Spire, and Rocky pressed all those buttons? They changed from green to red, remember? What if they controlled the RAZERs?'

Rockwell turned to look at Little-Bit. He could smell a hero moment.

'Er, yes,' he said. 'She's probably right. I mean, she's always right, isn't she? It must have been me. Basically, I disabled all of the RAZERs and saved us all. Yes. That is *definitely* what happened.'

The Jones sisters looked at each other and laughed fondly at Rockwell.

'Right, we need to start our descent,' said Peanut. 'Rockwell, do the honours. I can see normal trees and grass over there.'

He pulled the parachute-valve chord and

the balloon began to sink in the painted sky, resplendent in the kinds of reds, oranges and pinks that accompany the most beautiful sunsets. The deserts of Dali Point West were soon replaced by the rolling hills of the Green Valleys, and a few minutes later they spotted the winding river that led to the hay wain and the new Bunker.

'Peanut,' said Little-Bit, looking up at her big sister as they descended. 'I'm worried about Mum and Leo. Remember what the Markmakers said about our family being in danger now that Mr White knows about Dad probably being Conté's heir?'

'Listen, LB,' said Peanut, putting an arm around the little girl, 'that was before we got Little Tail back. Mr White is nowhere near Mum right now. He and Alan are still trying to get back to Chroma from New York, and then he'll only be thinking about how he's going to get his hands on the pencil again. So if anyone needs to be worried it's probably us. I'm sure he's not thinking about Mum and Leo at the moment. Anyway, we'll be back home soon, and we'll have Little Tail with us, so we can make sure that they're safe.'

'OK,' said Little-Bit, reassured. She snuggled into her big sister's embrace.

'Don't worry, guys,' said Rockwell as he guided the balloon smoothly downwards towards the red mill building. 'You've got me to protect you too, remember. And, as we have just established, I am a bona fide hero.'

37
Back in The Bunker

The balloon landed with a jolt in the field just behind the red mill building. The three children jumped out and made their way to the hay wagon Bunker entrance in the middle of the river. They ran down the stairs and straight into the room marked 'Transport'. Peanut was immediately struck by the number of people that were in there. It was busy the first time they'd visited, but this was something else.

Suddenly, a familiar bark rang through the air, shortly followed by a very excited Doodle, who ran to greet the children.

'Peanut! Rockwell! Little-Bit! There

you are!' shouted a cross-looking Mrs Markmaker, running towards them from behind an exquisitely drawn Chinook helicopter. 'What on earth happened? Where have you been? I've been worried sick!'

'I'm so sorry,' said Peanut. She'd never seen Mrs M looking angry before. 'I-I know we were reckless and what we did was dangerous. And I know you told us to stay where we were. The last thing we wanted was for you to worry, but I think it was a risk worth tak—'

'I need to find Malcolm and let him know that the three of you are safe,' interrupted Mrs M. 'He's been so worried.' She put her hands on Peanut's shoulders and squeezed them hard, before turning and heading out of the room.

'Where did all these extra Resistance people come from?' asked Rockwell, pushing a very licky Doodle away from his face. 'There are so many of them.'

'I was thinking the same thing,' replied Peanut, 'It's like . . .'

Mrs M came running back in with her husband. Following them was a tall, statuesque woman with razor-sharp cheekbones and short, white hair.

'Children!' said a breathless Mr M. 'What were you thinking? You've had us on pins and needles! You should have done as you were told and stayed in the Map Room.'

'I know,' said Peanut, 'And I'm really sorry, but—'

'I think,' said Mrs M, 'that you need to tell us exactly where you've been. And we need to fill you in on one or two things that have happened here too.'

The six of them sat at the round table in the Map Room, and Peanut told the Markmakers and the lady with the cheekbones everything. She explained how they'd snuck through the North Draw portal which led to the Louvre, and how they'd witnessed Mr White rubbing out the door in the plinth of the *Venus de Milo*.

'As we thought,' said Mr M, nodding. 'He's definitely shutting down the routes into and out of the city.'

Peanut described following Mr White through the catacombs and explained how they'd found Conté's grave and realised that it too was a portal. The Markmakers shifted in their seats as she described arriving in the Mission Control room at the top of the Spire, and finding a trapdoor leading to a swimming pool full of rainbow-coloured water. She told them about the doors drawn on the wall, and how one of those doors led them to New York. Mr and Mrs M looked horrified when she described jumping from the top of the Empire State Building.

'But . . . how did you draw a jet-pack?' asked Mr M,

frowning. 'Regular art equipment doesn't work like that in the real world. The only pencil with that power is . . .' His voice trailed off and his eyes narrowed behind his huge glasses.

Peanut smiled. Slowly, she pulled Little Tail from her bandolier and held it out towards Mr M. The silver-haired man's frown instantly disappeared and was replaced by a wide smile.

'Pencil Number One? Peanut! This is . . . amazing! How on earth . . . ? I mean, what did you . . . ? This is just . . .'

'Well, I'll be . . .' said Mrs M.

'We were hoping,' said Peanut, looking at Rockwell and Little-Bit, 'that when you realised we'd managed to get Little Tail back, you'd agree that the risk we took when we went through the North Draw portal was one that was worth taking. And that you'd forgive us.'

The Markmakers smiled.

'The three of you really are quite remarkable children,' said Mrs M. 'Full of surprises.'

'Speaking of surprises,' said Rockwell, 'Do you know why those horrible robots have all stopped working? It's because of me! I turned them all off when we were in the Mission

Control room at the top of the Spire! OK, so I didn't do it on purpose, but I did it nevertheless. Pretty good, huh?'

'Ah, that explains it!' said Mrs M. 'We wondered how that had happened.'

'I think this might be an appropriate moment to introduce myself,' said the lady with the cheekbones in a deep voice. 'My name is Josephine Engelberger, and I am the person who designed and built the RAZERs.'

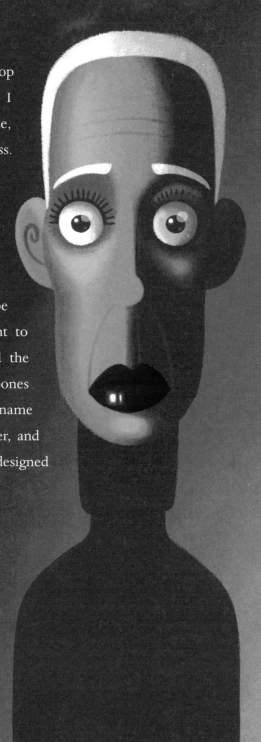

38
Josephine Engelberger

Peanut stood up, 'So you worked with Mr White?' she said, a tide of anger rising inside her. 'You helped him on his mission to destroy Chroma?'

'In a manner of speaking,' replied Engelberger.

Peanut spun around to face the Markmakers, her face bright red. 'WHY HAVE YOU LET THIS WOMAN INTO THE BUNKER? HOW DOES SHE EVEN KNOW WHERE THE BUNKER IS? SHE IS ON *HIS* SIDE!'

'Peanut,' said Mrs M calmly, 'Josephine is most definitely *not* on his side. On the contrary. She has been imprisoned in the Spire for the last twenty years, on Mr White's orders.'

Peanut stood staring at Engelberger, breathing hard. She could feel her heart racing. 'I, er, how . . . er, wh-why did he put you in prison?'

'Because,' said the woman, her voice low and measured, 'I dared to question him.'

'Question him how?' asked Little-Bit, eyeing the woman suspiciously.

'I questioned his motives for wanting the robots,' she replied. 'When he initially asked me to design them, I was led to believe that they would be serving Chroma. That they'd be a force for good and enhance the city's creative output.'

'Why on earth did you think that?' asked Peanut.

'Because that's what White told me,' she replied, tears pooling in her eyes. 'It seems ridiculous now, I grant you. But . . . I believed him.'

'We all did,' said Mrs M putting a hand on Engelberger's shoulder.

'So, hang on. You're a science person like me,' said Rockwell. 'Well, I must say it would be nice to have a scientific thinker to keep me company among all these creatives!'

'But, my friend, I am a creative person too,' said Engelberger, looking at the boy. 'I have swum in the Rainbow Lake. It just so happens that my gift is a knowledge and application of physics, engineering and, specifically, robotics.'

Peanut looked at Rockwell and shook her head. 'You're just like my mum. You have to stop with this whole *science versus art* thing. We've talked about this before. Don't you remember what Albert Einstein said?'

Rockwell frowned. 'He . . . he said that the greatest scientists are always artists as well.'

'Exactly!' said Little-Bit. 'Newton was a painter. Galileo was a poet . . .'

'She's right,' said Peanut, smiling now. 'Think of Leonardo da Vinci. He was pretty decent with a paintbrush, right? But he also knew a thing or two about engineering. The two aren't mutually exclusive.'

'Scientific endeavour is totally dependent on the huge leaps of imagination at its very core,' said Engelberger, nodding. 'You should never forget that, young man.'

'So what happened when you questioned Mr White?' said Peanut, who was now sitting back down in her chair.

'We had just finished building the first generation of RAZERs. I was excited to unveil them to Chroma's citizens. As far as I was concerned, they were going to be working on things like increasing pigment production, colour-correcting the Rainbow Lake, and helping to build the new galleries that we'd been planning for years. I thought the future of the city looked very bright at that point. But the first thing White sent them to do was to whitewash the famous Graffitied Wall in Warholia.'

'Oh! I think we just flew over that!' said Rockwell excitedly.

'I was appalled!' said Engelberger. 'I immediately went to see White, and I asked, in no uncertain terms, what he was up to. And right there, in the Mission Control room at the top of the tower, he revealed his true self to me for the first time. It was scary. Let's just say that he didn't like being questioned. Not at all! That was when I realised that the city had a big problem, and that I had contributed to it.'

'So what did you do?' asked Peanut.

'Well, I felt awful. Terribly guilty. But there was no time for self-pity. We were already working on the second generation of RAZER by that point, so I focused all of my energy on trying to program them to develop more autonomy. I wanted the robots themselves to be able to make decisions. I figured that at least that might help at some point in the future.'

The three children looked at each other.

'72!' they said in unison, remembering the rogue RAZER and Resistance operative who had helped them on Die Brücke, sacrificing themself by deliberately falling into the Rainbow Lake and causing a distraction so that the children could carry out their mission successfully.

'By then I knew I wouldn't be part of Mr White's regime for much longer. Not now that I had openly questioned his methods,' continued Engelberger. 'And, sure enough, a week later a platoon of RAZERs arrived at my lab in Modernia and took me to the Spire. I was imprisoned by the very robots that I had designed.' She smiled and shook her head. 'The irony.'

'Tell them, Josephine,' said Mr M. 'Tell the children what you've just told us. Tell them what you found out before you were imprisoned.'

'OK,' said the woman, taking a deep breath. 'In the week before I was taken to the Spire, White became much more vocal in terms of what he *really* wanted to achieve as Mayor of Chroma.'

'That he wants to mono the city and stop people from our world visiting Chroma?' asked Peanut.

'Yes. But that's just the start,' said Josephine. 'He also plans to drain the Rainbow Lake completely so that no one, from *any* world, will ever swim in it again. He wants to make sure that *all* creativity will die everywhere.'

39

Mr White's Masterplan

W h-whoa!' stammered Rockwell. 'Excuse me?'

'He wants to drain the Rainbow Lake.'

'I don't understand,' said Rockwell.

'I do,' said Peanut. 'He knows that the best way to destroy something is to stop it at its source, and the source of all the world's creativity is . . .'

'The Rainbow Lake,' finished Rockwell.

'Exactly,' continued Peanut. 'So if no one ever gets to swim in the Rainbow Lake again, well, not only will we say goodbye to future paintings and future artists, but also to every single other thing that requires creativity. Like comic books. And video games. Episodes of your favourite TV shows. Cartoons and memes. Fashion design. Trainers. Even stuff like doughnut flavours. Someone has to think up raspberry jam with salted caramel icing and sprinkles, you know. And what about—'

Rockwell held up his hand to stop her, eyebrows raised as the penny finally dropped. 'So what you're saying is . . .' He paused and swallowed hard. 'Unless we can stop Mr White, everything fun that life has to offer will disappear. Forever.'

'By George, I think he's got it,' said Little-Bit.

'But Mr White didn't account for the three of you,' said Mr M, smiling. 'You have struck a hugely important blow

already. By retrieving Little Tail you have given us hope. Yes, he has done a lot of damage by destroying so many of the portals and starting to mono the Illustrated City, but at least now we have a *chance* to stop him.'

Engelberger nodded. 'Agreed. We have to seize our opportunity.'

'We have to act *now!*' said Mrs M. 'We must fight back by seizing White's Mission Control room in the Spire. And we must keep the Rainbow Lake safe. When Mr White returns from New York, he will immediately restart the RAZERs, so we need to stop him before he does that. He'll be back in just a few hours. We don't have much time!'

'Yes,' agreed Mr M. 'Ladies and gentleman, we must initiate Operation Renaissance, and we must do it this second. There is no time to lose.'

40
Operation Renaissance

As the group walked from the Map Room to the Transport Room, Mr and Mrs Markmaker started shouting urgent instructions about 'Operation Renaissance' into their walkie-talkies, causing much frantic activity around them.

'Josephine,' said Peanut as they made their way towards the Transport Room. 'How did you escape from the Spire?'

'It was the strangest thing,' said Engelberger. 'Suddenly the doors to every single cell just . . . opened. It happened at exactly the same time that the RAZERs were disabled.' She looked over at Rockwell. 'So I am guessing that was also down to you and your button-pressing. Thank you, my friend.'

Rockwell grinned and looked down at Little-Bit. She smiled and held up her hand in readiness for the high-five that arrived with a satisfying slap.

'That explains why there are so many more people here helping the Resistance now, I guess,' said Peanut, looking at the hundreds of operatives running this way and that around the Bunker.

'Yes,' said Engelberger. 'It didn't take long for word of the new HQ to spread. If anybody has reason to want to stop that man, it is the people that he locked up in the Spire. It's a strong motivator, let me tell you. Quite a few of us came straight here, and I suspect there will be more joining us on the battlefield later.

We have a proper army at our disposal now.'

Peanut couldn't help but think of her father. If he hadn't escaped from the Spire, he might be there with them too. *Where are you, Dad?* she thought to herself. *And why aren't you coming to help? We need you. I need you. I wish, wish, WISH I could see you again and talk to you about what's been going on.*

'Sorry, did you just say "battlefield"?' said Rockwell, the smile disappearing from his face.

'Yes,' said Engelberger. 'Operation Renaissance is, essentially, our code name for the battle.'

Suddenly, the sound of a hundred engines igniting at the same time filled the bunker. Bright blue and pink military vehicles of all kinds revved their illustrated motors and got ready to roll.

'ALL UNITS, THIS IS ZERO ALPHA,' shouted Mrs M into her walkie-talkie. 'DEPLOY MUNITIONS. STAND BY TO ADVANCE ON OBJECTIVE SPIRE AT TWENTY-ONE HUNDRED HOURS. OUT.'

'Sorry, Mrs M,' said Rockwell. 'Er, can I just check? Josephine mentioned the word "battle" again just then. That doesn't mean we are going to be actually having, like, a proper *fight*, does it?'

Mrs M looked at him. 'I'm afraid it does rather, yes. But you three don't need to be here. You have done more than enough already. You should get back home. Peanut, I think you and Little-Bit need to be with your mother and your brother. You have to make sure that your family is safe.'

'But they are safe. Mr White . . . er, Mr Stone is not going to be concerned with Mum right now, anyway. He has other things on his mind. Plus, I have Little Tail now. If you think we're not going to stay and help after everything that has happened, well I'm afraid you've got another think coming,' said Peanut. 'Don't worry, we'll go back once the battle is won, but winning the battle is probably the best

chance we'll ever get to keep *everyone* safe – not just Mum and Leo.'

Mrs M nodded and stood up straight. She looked out of the huge doors that were slowly opening at the far end of the Transport Room to reveal a beautiful, starlit landscape with a tall, white spike at its centre.

'Well, children,' she said, 'in that case you'd better brace yourselves. Because the battle for control of the Spire is about to begin.'

41

The Battle for The Spire

'What are *munitions?*' said Little-Bit an hour later, as the three children and Doodle climbed into the back of their designated bright blue transporter truck and took their place on the bench seats.

'It's the posh word for *weapons,*' said Rockwell, 'which, in this case, appear to consist almost entirely of art equipment.'

Peanut raised her hand to her bandolier, where Little Tail sat safely in its slot. She was determined that the two of them wouldn't be separated ever again.

The children were sitting opposite the Resistance agents who had been charged with their protection. On the left was a very cute-looking koala called Tony, dressed in full camouflage gear. He already seemed quite amped for the upcoming action, and was repeatedly slapping himself around the face and shouting things like 'COME ON!' and 'YOU CAN DO THIS!' Next to him was a colourful, if slightly abstract-looking woman called Dora, who was handing out pink and blue ink-bomb belts. She was also distributing pairs of small, bud-style earphones which she told the children they must wear at all times.

Just as they were putting them into their ears, the truck started to move. Peanut looked out through the windows at the convoy of vehicles surrounding them. It was an impressive sight. There were a number of large, illustrated tanks – not quite in the same league as the Big Xs, but intimidating nevertheless – in addition to jeeps, lorries, trucks and a host of small armoured cars. Immediately in front of them were three open-topped hovercraft, being driven by Mrs M, Mr M and Josephine Engelberger. As the platoon of vehicles made their way out through the large hangar doors and into the crisp night air of the Green Valleys, Peanut turned to look back at

the Bunker. It appeared that the entire hillside had opened up
to let them out.

'Oooh, it's just like the Batcave,' said Rockwell.

The strange motorcade, now joined by several low-flying
aircraft, made its way through the moonlit countryside of the
Green Valleys, iridescent in indigos, purples and violets. In the
distance, they could see the Spire rising, luminous, in the night
sky like a beacon of hope or a harbinger of doom, depending
on which way you looked at it.

'ALL UNITS, THIS IS ZERO BETA . . .'

The three children jumped as Mr M's voice rang loudly in
their ears. Dora, the abstract lady, smiled.

'ESTIMATED TIME ON OBJECTIVE SPIRE IS
TWENTY-THREE HUNDRED HOURS. SIEGE TOWER
ENGINEERS, PREPARE TO MOVE IN FORTY-FIVE. OUT.'

'Mr and Mrs M will direct the battle via our headsets,'
explained Dora. 'It's how we'll coordinate the operation and

make sure everyone is doing what they should be doing at the right time.'

'So I guess this is really happening,' said Rockwell in a resigned tone.

'Don't worry,' said Peanut. 'We'll be fine. Remember what the Markmakers said during the briefing: we won't be on the front line. Hopefully the Spire will be recaptured before Mr White and Alan return from New York and turn the RAZERs back on, so we won't have any opposition. The Resistance just have to cross the lake, get past the crayon fence, and then enter the tower as quickly as possible. That way, when White and Alan do get back, our operatives will be waiting to arrest them. And by then, you'll be back home with a nice cup of tea, reading *Aerospace Engineering and the Principle of Flight*.'

'Ah, that *would* be nice,' said Rockwell, 'but somehow, I don't think it's going to be that easy. Things in Chroma

42
The Siege Tower

As the convoy approached the Spire, they were greeted by the intimidating sight of a Big X pointing straight towards them, surrounded by several inactive platoons of RAZERs. To the left and right, a number of equally imposing Big Xs sat in a circular formation around the edge of the lake, each one facing out towards a district of the city and flanked by more dormant RAZER platoons. Peanut noticed that there were also two robots sitting in each Big X cockpit, their eyes, thankfully, dark. The Rainbow Lake itself, resplendent in its perfectly striped, multicoloured glory, shimmered in the moonlight, and just beyond that, the enormous white Spire rose majestically into the night sky.

'Thank goodness the RAZERs have been deactivated,'

said Rockwell. 'I wouldn't fancy our chances otherwise.'

'Look. They've finished painting the crayon fence white now,' said Little-Bit sadly. 'And they've started monoing all of the districts.'

She was right. The first hundred metres of each district was now entirely without colour. This made the lake look even more vibrant, although Peanut noticed that the water level was considerably lower than it had been the last time she had seen it. The Markmakers had warned her what to expect, but it was still a shock to see the beautiful Rainbow Lake only about three-quarters full.

'Yeah, but look at how many of us are here now to put a stop to all that stuff,' said Rockwell, turning towards the

impressive convoy behind them. 'Josephine was right, our numbers really have swollen. I don't want to tempt fate, but I think we're actually going to do this.'

He turned back to Peanut, who was suddenly looking very worried. 'Er, what's wrong?'

'The drawbridge. It's raised,' she replied, her brow furrowed. 'And we need to get our operatives and vehicles across the lake as quickly as possible. It'll take ages for people to fly or swim over and lower the bridge by hand. That could well mean that Mr White and Alan will get back before we can get anywhere near Mission Control.'

'I bet the Markmakers will have known that this might happen,' said Little-Bit calmly. 'They'll have it covered. I know it.'

'What do you reckon they're going to do?' asked Rockwell.

'I think we're about to find out,' said Peanut.

Suddenly a familiar voice sounded in their ears. 'ALL UNITS, THIS IS ZERO ALPHA,' said Mrs M. 'H MINUS ONE MINUTE. PREPARE TO LAUNCH OPERATION RENAISSANCE! SIEGE TOWER ENGINEERS, STAND BY TO MOVE. OUT.'

A large and very pink lorry emerged from the pack, drove on to the concrete expanse that surrounded the Spire, and stopped about ten metres in front of the powered-down

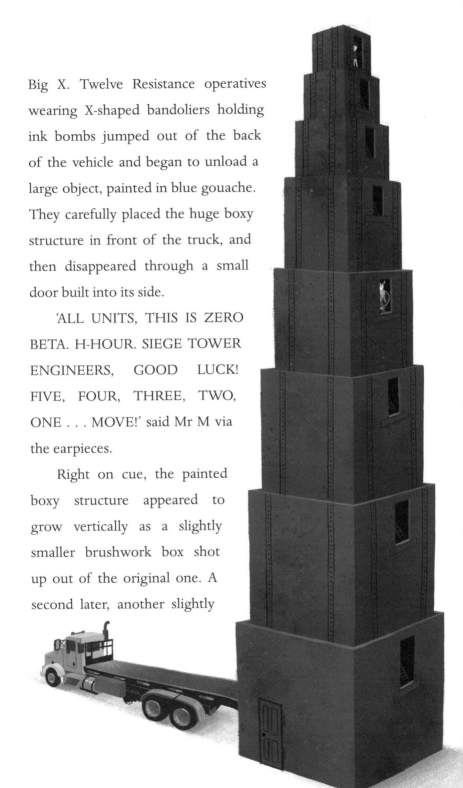

Big X. Twelve Resistance operatives wearing X-shaped bandoliers holding ink bombs jumped out of the back of the vehicle and began to unload a large object, painted in blue gouache. They carefully placed the huge boxy structure in front of the truck, and then disappeared through a small door built into its side.

'ALL UNITS, THIS IS ZERO BETA. H-HOUR. SIEGE TOWER ENGINEERS, GOOD LUCK! FIVE, FOUR, THREE, TWO, ONE . . . MOVE!' said Mr M via the earpieces.

Right on cue, the painted boxy structure appeared to grow vertically as a slightly smaller brushwork box shot up out of the original one. A second later, another slightly smaller one shot up out of that. Then another, and another. This continued until the ingenious, tapering, telescopic tower had risen to a height of around thirty metres. Each level had a large opening cut into its side, through which the Resistance operatives could be seen climbing ladders as they made their way up the inside of the tower. Half of the operatives stopped at an open doorway ten metres from the top, and the other half went right to the summit.

The children stared through the windows, open-mouthed at the rapidly erected tower.

'That was SO cool,' said Little-Bit.

'Classic Roman ingenuity,' said Rockwell.

'Amazing,' said Peanut. 'But what are they going to do now?'

'Well, they'll need some sort of gangplank to get across to the Spire. But first they'll have to breach its walls. I'm guessing they'll use some sort of trebuchet.'

'What does "breach" mean?' asked Peanut.

'Make a big hole,' he replied.

'Ah. So this is how they'll get people into the Spire without having to lower the drawbridge,' said a smiling Peanut.

'I knew they'd have a plan,' said Little-Bit. 'Er, Rocky. What's a trebuchet?'

Rockwell grinned. 'Peanut, can you write today's date down please? It's a momentous occasion. I want to remember it as the day that I knew something that LB didn't.'

An Awakening

'S o a trebuchet is a giant catapult?' said Little-Bit, looking at the lengthy pink-and-blue contraption that was being towed into position twenty metres behind the siege tower.

'Essentially, yes,' replied Rockwell, revelling in his position as the resident expert on proceedings. 'As you can see, they're comprised of a long arm with a cradle to hold the projectile on one end, and then a big box full of something very heavy at the other. The heavy end is then winched up really high, and when you drop it back down, it whips the arm around to throw the projectile. They're pretty awesome, to be honest, but they take a while to set up because they're so big.'

'Well, I wish they'd get a move on,' said Peanut, looking at

her watch. 'Mr White and Alan could be back any second now.'

The children watched as a team of hamsters wearing bright blue helmets ran into a giant wheel at the base of the trebuchet and started running furiously, causing it to spin. This set the whole mechanism in motion so that the large box at one end of the giant arm began to slowly rise up, and the cradle at the other started to descend. As the cradle approached the ground, several Resistance agents began to roll an extremely dense charcoal missile towards the cradle.

That's when it happened.

An ear-splitting roar filled the skies all around the

Rainbow Lake. It was so loud that the buds popped out of Rockwell's ears, and the hamsters operating the trebuchet instantly froze. Peanut felt a familiar but unwelcome fluttering sensation in the pit of her stomach as the truck they were sitting in began to vibrate. Everybody looked towards the source of the noise.

Long plumes of black smoke had started to emerge from the five chimneys on top of the Big X, and, to the horror of the children, the eyes of the RAZERs in the cockpit were glowing red.

Peanut swallowed hard. 'They're back.'

44
'Loose!'

The Big X finished its deafeningly loud ignition cycle and, piloted by the newly revived RAZERs, started to move slowly, but ominously, towards the Resistance.

Peanut stood up and reached for Little Tail, but was immediately told to sit back down by Tony and Dora.

'Our orders are to make sure you're safe at all times,' said the woman.

'But Mr White and Alan must have arrived back in Chroma!' shouted Peanut.

'I'm sorry, but you can't be directly involved in combat. It's too big a risk.'

Reluctantly, Peanut sat down, but made sure to check that the canvas flap at the rear of the truck wasn't tied shut. Meanwhile, a panicky Rockwell picked up his dropped earbuds from the floor of the truck and put them back in just in time to hear Mrs M shout, 'ARCHERS, IN POSITION!'

Dozens of Resistance operatives emerged from canvas-covered transporters and arranged themselves, with military precision, into a large crescent shape just ahead of the convoy. Each one was carrying a large graphite longbow and wearing a narrow quiver fully stocked with neatly drawn arrows. Then a second wave of artillery operatives appeared, carrying tins of pink and blue paint which they placed in front of each archer. A third and final wave followed, this time carrying crossbows. They knelt just behind the first wave that was now making up the front line.

'NOCK!' bellowed Mrs M.

In perfect unison, the standing archers took an arrow from their quivers, loaded it on to their bowstrings, and drew them back.

'DIP!'

They leaned forward at a forty-five-degree angle and

dipped the tips of the arrows into the paint tins.

'AIM!'

They leaned back.

'LOOSE!'

The archers let fly. The volley of colourful arrows flew high through the air, leaving a perfect arc of speckly pink and blue paint droplets in its wake. They soared past the siege tower and over the slow-moving Big X, clearing the Rainbow Lake and the crayon fence before exploding in a riot of colour against the white wall of the Spire. Peanut's heart leaped. The sight of the previously pristine building getting splattered was extremely powerful, and it restored some of the hope that had disappeared when she'd seen the Big X and RAZERs come back to life.

A few seconds later, the kneeling second wave of archers stood up and, as one, moved smoothly past the first, taking the tins of paint with them.

'NOCK!'

They knelt back down and loaded their crossbows.

'DIP!'

They dipped their bolts in the paint.

'AIM!'

This time they kept their bows low.

'LOOSE!'

The paint-covered bolts flew horizontally across the open concrete plain and hit their targets hard, smashing into the Big X and the RAZER platoons, turning them a fetching shade of pinky blue and knocking several of the robots clean over.

'Nice shooting!' shouted Little-Bit.

'It didn't work though,' said Rockwell. 'Look!'

Sure enough, the gigantic Big X was still advancing menacingly towards them, flanked by the remaining RAZERs on either side.

'INFANTRY, TARGET TO YOUR FRONT. ENGAGE! AIR DIVISION, ENGAGE BIG X! TAKE HIM OUT!' ordered Mr M, a more urgent tone to his voice.

Another deployment of brave soldiers raced forward and started to paint several enormous spiky anti-tank obstacles known as Czech hedgehogs. They were working a few metres in front of the archers, who were preparing to fire another high volley at the Spire.

Suddenly the children felt a strong downdraught as three Resistance helicopters from the rear of the convoy flew over them. They hovered directly over the advancing Big X and started to drop a barrage of ink bombs. Several RAZERs were disabled by the inky explosions, but the huge vehicle was unaffected. It just kept rolling forwards on its gigantic tracks.

'They'll never stop it,' howled Rockwell. 'We're done for!'

'Nonsense!' shouted Peanut, who was itching to get involved in the action. 'We just need to strike harder ourselves. Surely attack is the best form of defence!'

'Don't forget the trebuchet and the siege towers,' said Little-Bit, surveying the battleground. 'We've still got those and they're ready to go!'

45
Breaching the Spire

'ARTILLERY, PREPARE TO FIRE!' shouted Mrs M in their headphones.

Several Resistance operatives pushed the giant charcoal missile into the trebuchet's cradle, stepped back and held their arms aloft. The hamsters emerged from inside the wheel and did the same.

'READY . . . FIRE!'

A white rabbit wearing red dungarees pulled a lever at the machine's base, and the trebuchet sprang into action, whipping the arm up and over, and flinging the round missile towards the Spire at a frightening speed. A few seconds later it hit the tower twenty metres from the ground, smashing through the brickwork and making a large hole in its wall.

'WHOA!' shouted Little-Bit. 'That was INCREDIBLE!'

'And look over there!' cried Rockwell, pointing to their left.

They all turned to the siege tower and saw two horizontal walkways shooting out of the raised doorways. They extended rapidly through the air towards the Spire, the lower one meeting the newly made hole in the wall perfectly.

'Nice!' said an appreciative Rockwell. 'I can only imagine the calculations that went into making that happen.'

The Resistance operatives who had been waiting patiently inside the siege tower ran out on to the walkways armed with the ink bombs from their bandoliers. At the same time, several RAZERs appeared at the hole in the Spire at the other end and also began to make their way across.

'Oh my goodness, they're going to meet in the middle!' said Little-Bit.

'Looks like it,' said Peanut. She glanced over at Dora and Tony, who were standing near the cabin of the truck

and looking out of the window, mesmerised by what was happening on the battlefield.

Meanwhile, the agents on the siege tower's upper walkway had started raining ink bombs down on the RAZERs below them. Three of the robots took a direct hit and were knocked off balance, falling into the Rainbow Lake with a fizz of electricity and a puff of smoke. The rest of them continued advancing towards the Resistance operatives, who were being led by a heavily muscled man wearing a Viking helmet and carrying a huge missile launcher.

'It's Agent Odin the Stormbreaker!' said Rockwell. 'He must have escaped from the Spire!'

All of a sudden, the agent stopped running, knelt down and raised the bazooka to his shoulder.

'PRINCIPLE. DROP ONE HUNDRED. RIGHT ONE HUNDRED. PREPARE TO FIRE,' came the order over the earpieces. Agent Odin the Stormbreaker

adjusted his aim slightly, as directed.

'READY . . . FIRE!' said Mr M via the earpieces.

A massive blast of pink and blue paint flew towards the remaining RAZERs, totally drenching them. Two fell from the walkway into the water, while the others stopped dead and attempted to clear the paint from their eyes with tiny wiper blades that dropped down from their helmets.

'Come on,' said Peanut. 'This looks like a good time to make a break for it.'

'Excuse me?' whispered Rockwell. 'You heard what Dora said. We're meant to stay right here!'

Peanut turned to face her friend. 'Listen. Not only do I have a whole bandolier full of art equipment, but I also happen to be in possession of the most powerful pencil in the world. Those fighters out there need all the help they can get, and I am going to offer some. We've got to do something! Come on, let's go!'

Checking to make sure that Dora and Tony were still distracted by the battle, Peanut, Rockwell and Little-Bit went through the open canvas flap, jumped off the back of the truck and ran towards an old-fashioned motorbike and sidecar parked behind a small tank a few metres away.

'This'll do,' said Peanut, leaping on the bike. 'Come on, you two!'

Rockwell and Little-Bit jumped into the sidecar as Peanut started the engine and zoomed off towards the front. They weaved between the empty vehicles, and stopped a couple of minutes later behind the lorry that had been carrying the siege tower.

'OK. Rockwell, get the jumpsuits out,' said Peanut as she got off the bike.

'Seriously? They were only to be used in case of emergency!' he replied, reaching inside his rucksack.

'Er, we need a disguise if we don't want the Markmakers to send us straight back to the truck,' she replied. 'If this isn't an emergency, I don't know what is!'

Rockwell pulled out several hand-painted items, all made by Peanut just before they'd left the bunker. The children slipped the camouflage jumpsuits on over their clothes and put on the sunglasses. Peanut then pulled a piece of charcoal from her bandolier and drew thick black lines across their cheeks.

'Right, commandos,' she said. 'Time to win this battle.'

46

Friends Reunited

eanut made her way around the siege-tower lorry, closely followed by Rockwell and Little-Bit. The noise on the front line was incredible – the *thwup-thwup* of helicopter blades, the *whoosh* of flying arrows, the splash of exploding ink bombs, all underpinned by the thundering roar of the approaching Big X. Peanut thought that the Resistance's task seemed even more impossible when viewed at close quarters.

The area immediately behind the archers was a hive of activity. Paint-splattered Resistance operatives were being tended to, weapons were being repaired, and the siege equipment was being fortified. The hamsters were back in the wheel, lowering the trebuchet cradle as quickly as

they could, while operatives prepared
another charcoal missile. Peanut spotted
the Markmakers and Josephine looking anxious ten
metres to their left. They were studying a large sheet of
paper and talking animatedly. She got the impression that the
battle wasn't going very well.

'DOODLE!' shouted Little-Bit, suddenly running towards
a small figure that emerged from a group of soldiers to their
left. Sure enough, it was their canine friend, wearing a flak
jacket, a helmet with the word 'AMMUNITION' stencilled
across it, and carrying a fresh tin of paint in his mouth. He put
down the tin and wagged his tail when he saw the children,
who all made a big fuss of him.

'It's great to see you, boy,' said Little-Bit. Even Rockwell welcomed the licks, mainly because they momentarily took his mind off the fact that were in the middle of a huge battle that they couldn't possibly win.

'I am sure you lot aren't meant to be here,' said a soft, friendly voice behind them. The four of them turned around and were greeted by a sight that made them smile ear to ear.

'JONATHAN HIGGINBOTTOM!' they said in unison.

47
Peanut Has an Idea

The very same,' said the enormous alligator, who they had initially encountered during their first visit to Chroma. He was wearing a white armband with a red cross on it, which, Peanut figured, meant that he was part of the medical corps.

'Now,' continued Jonathan Higginbottom, 'I know for a fact that you three are not meant to be anywhere near the front line, but somehow I'm not remotely surprised to see you here. And as for those disguises, well let's just say they need a little work.'

'Please don't tell on us,' said Peanut. 'We're here because I genuinely think Little Tail and I can help.'

Suddenly there was a loud cry above them. They looked up to see one of the Resistance operatives, who had been fighting the RAZERs, fall from the siege-tower walkway and plunge into the Rainbow Lake. A few seconds later, to everyone's relief, her head bobbed up to the surface and she started swimming towards the concrete bank on the far side. Peanut noticed that the woman was moving through the water with real purpose. Eventually, she reached the bank and climbed up the metal rungs embedded in the concrete wall. Once out, she ran, unopposed, towards the big wheel next to the raised drawbridge, grabbed the handle and, to Peanut's delight, slowly started to lower the bridge.

That's when she had her idea.

'We have to break through the crayon fence!' she spluttered. 'If we can do that, we might be able to get into the Spire and make our way up to Mission Control at the top. Then we could turn off the Big X and the RAZERs, just like Rockwell did before.'

'How on earth are we going to break through the crayon fence, let alone all the other stuff?' asked Rockwell.

'*We're* not,' said Peanut, 'But Jonathan Higginbottom and I are.'

48
The Battering Ram Alligator

'Now what's she drawing?' shouted Rockwell over the hubbub as he watched Peanut sketching furiously.

'It looks like two pairs of roller boots,' said Little-Bit.

Doodle cocked his head to one side as Peanut put down her brush pen, picked up the circular stamp and started to print some wheels. When she'd finished, she handed the boots to Jonathan Higginbottom.

'Ooh, thank you,' said the alligator excitedly. 'I haven't skated since I was a hatchling. I used to love a good roller-disco!'

Peanut pulled Little Tail from her bandolier and drew two helmets: a small one that she put on her own head, and a much bigger one, with enormous horns on the sides.

'This is for you, too,' she said, handing it to Jonathan Higginbottom.

'So what are we going to do while you two try to break the crayon fence?' asked Little-Bit.

'I'm glad you asked,' smiled Peanut.

'We need you to create a diversion.'

49

The Diversion

'We look RIDICULOUS!' moaned Rockwell.

'That's kind of the point,' said Peanut, desperately trying to keep the smile from her face.

'Well, I LOVE it!' shouted Little-Bit. 'I've always wanted to have a go at this.'

'Right, there's no time to lose,' said Peanut. 'Jonathan Higginbottom, are you ready?'

'As I'll ever be,' he replied.

'OK. Positions, everyone,' said Peanut, as she clambered up on to the alligator's back and sat in the spray-painted saddle. 'And . . . GO!'

Little-Bit ran out from behind the startled archers and headed left. Rockwell and Doodle followed closely behind.

When they reached the end of the line, all three turned around, lifted their pompoms and faced the Big X. The two children took a deep breath and started to chant at the tops of their voices:

> *Two . . . four . . . six . . . eight . . .*
> *Who don't we appreciate?*
> RA-ZERs! Mr White!
> *You are gonna lose tonight!*

For a split second, everybody on the battlefield stopped what they were doing and looked over at the bizarre little troupe, their mouths agape. Even the RAZERs driving the Big X turned to view the dancing trio, stopping the vehicle while they took in the extraordinarily out-of-place scene. Rockwell and Little-Bit continued:

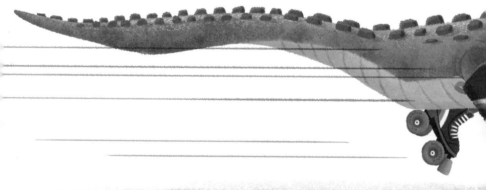

One . . . two . . . three . . . four . . .
We're Resistance, hear us roar!
Big X, RAZERs too,
You know what you gotta do . . .
GO! GO! GO!'

'They're all looking the other way! This is our chance!'
shouted Peanut. 'GO, JONATHAN HIGGINBOTTOM, GO!'

The alligator pushed off on all four skates with surprising
agility and started to glide elegantly across the concrete. 'Just
like riding a bike,' he said, as he flew past the archers and
skated around the Big X.

Peanut clung on to the painted reins as she and Jonathan Higginbottom sped towards the newly lowered drawbridge. She couldn't resist letting out a loud 'WHOO-HOO!'

After a couple of seconds, several of the RAZERs stopped staring at the cheerleaders and noticed the roller-skating alligator. They immediately set off in pursuit, but to no avail. With a flick of his tail, Jonathan Higginbottom skittled the few that got close, sending them sprawling across the concrete. The rest were left behind in his wake. He really was a fabulous skater!

As they reached the drawbridge, Peanut heard a distant chant of 'Higginbottom, he's our man! If he can't do it, no one can!' The alligator lowered his head as they thundered along, pointing the huge horns on his helmet directly towards the crayon fence at the far end of the bridge.

'Hold tight, young Peanut. Impact in approximately ten seconds . . .'

Peanut leaned forward so that her chest was flat against Jonathan Higginbottom's back and she too lowered her head.

'Five, four, three, two, one . . .'

CRASH!

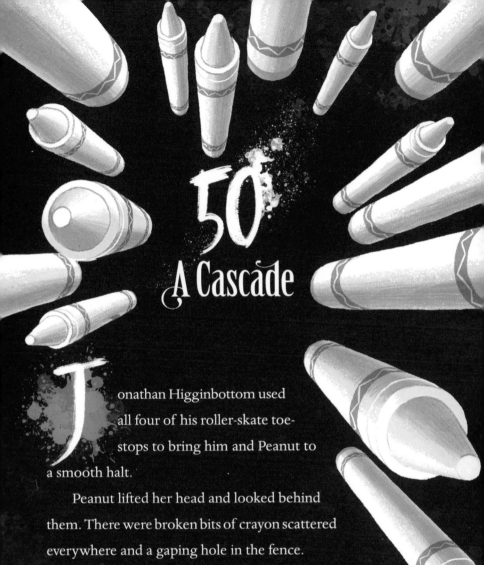

50
A Cascade

Jonathan Higginbottom used all four of his roller-skate toe-stops to bring him and Peanut to a smooth halt.

Peanut lifted her head and looked behind them. There were broken bits of crayon scattered everywhere and a gaping hole in the fence.

'We did it!' she shouted. 'Great work, Jonathan Higginbottom! Right, we need to get to the top of the Spire!'

'Indeed,' agreed the alligator, looking over at the battle that was, once again, raging on the other side of the lake. 'And we need to be quick.'

They turned and faced the towering building.

'Look! An entrance!' said Peanut, pointing. 'And the doors are open!'

'It's almost too easy,' said Jonathan Higginbottom.

Unfortunately, he had spoken too soon. Just as the words left his long, tooth-filled mouth, a cascade of RAZERs began to pour out of the doorway, accompanied by a seemingly never-ending shoal of Exocetia – the brassy, mechanical fish that Mr White used to hunt down his enemies.

'Oh dear,' said Jonathan Higginbottom, 'Slight problem . . .'

'QUICK! RUN, er . . . SKATE!' shouted Peanut.

But it was too late. They were completely surrounded.

51
'Hello, Alan'

Once the last of the Exocetia had funnelled out of the Spire and joined the thousands surrounding Peanut and Jonathan Higginbottom, a phalanx of twelve gleaming, golden RAZERs emerged and arranged themselves in a V-formation around the doorway.

A few seconds later, a tall figure with a neck as thick as his head appeared.

'Well, well, well,' he said. 'Long time no see, *little girl*.'

'Hello, *Alan*,' said Peanut. 'Hope you enjoyed your extended mini-break in New York. Have you come back to show us your holiday photos, or just to offer your surrender?'

The man laughed. 'On the contrary. It looks like the game is finally up for you and your little Resistance friends. Look.'

Peanut looked back through the hole in the crayon fence just in time to see the siege tower brought crashing to the ground by the Big X. The archers were retreating in panic and many of the vehicles in the convoy were wheel-spinning away from the front line. She hoped upon hope that Little-Bit and Rockwell were OK. She steeled herself and turned back to face Mr White's henchman.

'Let me tell you something,' she said, 'There is no way that I am going to be beaten by a man who is as annoying as you are, and whose suit is at least two sizes too small for him.'

'Actually,' said Alan, 'I'm afraid you don't really have any choice in the matter, so you can quit monkeying about.'

'Speaking of monkeys, where's the organ-grinder?' said Peanut, removing her helmet and shaking out her topknot.

'The *what*?' said Alan, dumbfounded.

'Oh, sorry. I forgot that I needed to spell things out for you,' said Peanut. 'I'm enquiring as to the whereabouts of your boss. You know, Mr White. The guy who makes all the *important* decisions. I could do with talking to someone with *real* influence right now.'

Alan's pale face flushed, and his freckles turned scarlet.

'Mr White is . . . otherwise engaged at present. But don't worry, because I can assure you that I am fully authorised to take charge in his absence.'

Peanut and Jonathan Higginbottom exchanged glances. Something about this didn't feel right. Why on earth would Mr White not be here to celebrate his moment of victory? After all, Alan did have a point. The battle did appear to be all but over.

'Face it, Jones,' continued Alan. 'Whatever it was that you and the Resistance were trying to achieve, it hasn't worked. You've failed.' As if on cue, a cloud drifted in front of the moon and the city got a little bit darker. 'Now, be a good kid and give me the pencil.'

Peanut looked down at her hand. She was holding Little Tail. Strangely, she had no memory of removing it from her bandolier.

'Come on. Any hope that stealing it gave you has now gone.'

Peanut looked at Alan. Then back down at the pencil. Then at Alan again.

'You're wrong,' she said coolly. 'Firstly, I didn't steal it. You can't steal something that is already yours. Secondly, there is *always* hope. I've learned that no matter how bleak things appear to be, any situation can be turned around.'

She looked up at the moon as it emerged from behind the cloud and recast its silvery light across Chroma. She thought she saw a silhouette of something fly across its face.

'In fact,' she continued, 'they say that the darkest hour is often the one just before dawn.'

Then, from above, an American-accented voice that Peanut instantly recognised spoke.

'I couldn't have said it better myself, citizen!'

52
The Cloaked Division

'Table Guy! Am I glad to see you!' said Peanut, smiling at the superhero wearing the dark brown spandex bodystocking, and standing on the large coffee table floating a couple of metres above her and Jonathan Higginbottom.

'Yes! It is I!' he replied. Peanut remembered that he only spoke in sentences ending in an exclamation mark.

'Can you get us out of here?' said Peanut.

'Of course I can! But first we must attend to this!' Table Guy nodded towards Alan. 'CAST YOUR NETS, FISHER MAN!'

An equally muscular figure, wearing thigh-length yellow boots and a yellow cape with built-in sou'wester, was sitting in a flying rowing boat that had just appeared out of nowhere. He stood up, adopted a wide-legged, heroic stance, and started firing some sort of webbing from his fingertips. The webbing merged together to form huge nets that floated down through the air and completely covered Alan, the RAZERs and the Exocetia.

'CATCH OF THE DAY!' shouted Fisher Man, with a chuckle.

'Thank you, Fisher Man!' shouted Peanut, before turning to Table Guy and beaming. 'Shall we?'

The superhero cleared his throat. 'BY THE WONDER OF WOOD!' he bellowed.

Seconds after he shouted the words, a very long table that looked like it must have come from the boardroom in a fancy office somewhere flew around from behind the Spire and floated gently down to the ground.

'Climb aboard, Mr Higginbottom!' said Table Guy. The alligator kicked off his roller skates and did as he was told. Peanut, meanwhile, clambered up on to Table Guy's flying coffee table and adopted a surfing stance.

'OK! LET'S FLY!' commanded Table Guy, and the pieces of furniture, with their passengers safely on board, soared high into the air.

'Table Guy, won't they be able to get out of those nets pretty easily?' asked Peanut.

'Don't worry!' he replied, as they flew towards the battleground. 'Cheese Girl and Inferno have got it covered!'

Peanut looked back to see yet another muscular superhero flying towards the Spire. She was wearing a pale-

yellow suit covered in an interesting, if slightly repulsive, blue veiny pattern, and she left a strong smell of Stilton in her wake. Flying just behind her was a man who appeared to be completely on fire. Peanut noticed that he was holding his nose as he flew.

The two heroes stopped in mid-air when they reached the Spire, hovering directly above the writhing mass of robots struggling to free themselves from Fisher Man's nets. They looked down and exchanged a few words, before Cheese Girl

proceeded to hold her hands ten centimetres apart, palms facing inwards. She started muttering a strange incantation, and, as she did so, a small pale-yellow ball materialised between her palms. It grew bigger and bigger as she moved her hands further apart. She kept going until it was about a metre in diameter. She then lowered her hands, leaving the strange object floating in the air, and backed away. At this point, Inferno moved into position and squared up to the floating cheese ball. He opened his mouth and (there's no other way to describe it) burped fire at it. A powerful blast of white-hot flame shot out and blasted the cheese, instantly melting it. The resulting thick, gloopy liquid rained down on the crowd below, totally covering them. Alan, the RAZERs and the Exocetia, who by this point were almost free from the netting, suddenly found themselves covered by a hot, stringy mess, and unable to move.

'I GUESS IT'S JUST *NACHO* DAY!' shouted Cheese Girl to the fromage-covered crowd.

'YEAH!' yelled Inferno. 'YOU GUYS NEED TO THINK *CAERPHILLY* ABOUT YOUR LIFE CHOICES!'

Peanut smiled and shook her head. 'What is it with superheroes and puns?' she said.

53
The Turn of the Tide

The sky over the Rainbow Lake was filled with superheroes flying towards the Green Valleys battlefield.

'I finally got through to them!' explained Table Guy. 'At first, they thought that a city full of unhappy people would lead to higher crime rates, which would mean more hero work for us! But my fellow supers eventually agreed that losing the heart of the city we love is not a price worth paying! The final straw was when the Big Xs started to plough through the districts! That's when they agreed to join me in helping the Resistance! And that's why we're here tonight!'

'Thank you,' said Peanut. 'So, who's that over there?'

'That's Badger Boy!' said Table Guy. 'A good friend! He

was standing near me at the back of the queue on power-giving day! I think he overslept too! Admittedly, a badger is not the first animal whose powers you'd like to be able to harness, but wait until you see what he can do with those claws! Especially when he's working alongside his counterparts, Mole Chap and The Earthworm!'

'And what about her?' asked Peanut, pointing to a woman flying to their left, dressed in bright red, with a selection of giant, foldable metal tools behind her back, fanning out like metallic angel's wings.

'That's Generic Multi-Functional Pocket Tool Girl!

A powerful ally in many different ways! Particularly if the mission requires you to file your nails or open a bottle of wine!'

Table Guy brought their flying coffee table to a stop and Jonathan Higginbottom pulled up next to them on his boardroom table. They watched as the heroes began to do their stuff.

Badger Boy swooped down towards the Big X that was carving its way through the remaining Resistance convoy. He was closely followed by a tall, thin man in a reddish-brown, ribbed costume, and a much shorter figure dressed entirely in black, with enormous silver claws and a silver visor covering his eyes. The Earthworm and Mole Chap, Peanut assumed. Badger Boy led them towards the grass area just in front of the Big X and, instead of slowing down as they neared the ground, he accelerated, before disappearing, claws first, with an explosion of earth, into the grassy hillside. A few seconds later all three heroes burst back out, via another muddy explosion about thirty metres away.

'What are they doing?' asked Jonathan Higginbottom.

'Watch, citizen!' said Table Guy.

Slowly, the ground between the heroes' entry and exit points started to move. It was hard to spot at first, but then the mini-landslide became more and more widespread. All of a sudden, it collapsed in on itself creating a huge trench about three metres wide and ten metres deep.

One of the Big X's strengths, its gargantuan size, was also its weakness. It meant that changing direction was a very slow process. Consequently, there was nothing the RAZERs in the cockpit could do to avoid what happened next. The massive vehicle plunged teeth first into the trench, tipping forwards a full ninety degrees, leaving its giant treads whirring uselessly in the air.

'YES!' yelled Peanut, as if she'd scored a goal at Wembley. 'IN YOUR FACE, BIG X!'

'Now it's time for Bucket Head to do his thing!' said Table Guy, pointing at another hero, whose head appeared to be a made of a large, slightly rusty bucket. 'Watch him go!'

The flying, bucket-headed man positioned himself directly over a particularly aggressive platoon of RAZERs who were outnumbering a cluster of archers by the fallen siege tower. He then proceeded to tip his head slowly forward. To Peanut and Jonathan Higginbottom's amazement, a huge torrent of water poured from his bucket, and splashed down on to the robots, causing them to instantly short-circuit. Bucket Head

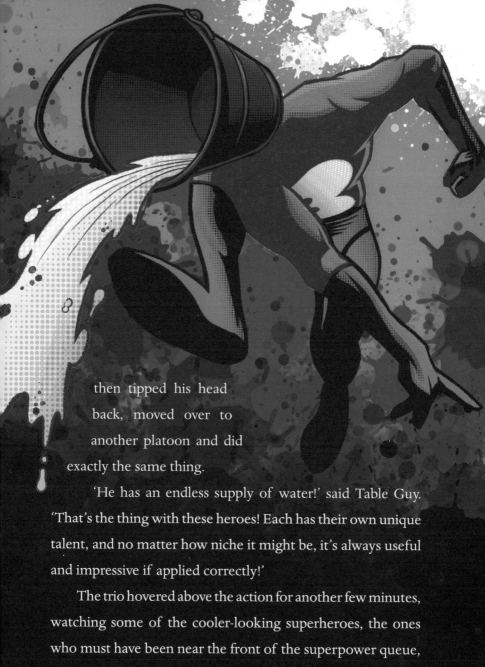

then tipped his head
back, moved over to
another platoon and did
exactly the same thing.

'He has an endless supply of water!' said Table Guy.
'That's the thing with these heroes! Each has their own unique
talent, and no matter how niche it might be, it's always useful
and impressive if applied correctly!'

The trio hovered above the action for another few minutes,
watching some of the cooler-looking superheroes, the ones
who must have been near the front of the superpower queue,
do their thing. Captain Chill was particularly effective with
her beautifully sculpted ice-statues of mermaids and unicorns

that temporarily came to life and chased the RAZERs into the same trench that claimed the Big X, before melting away to nothing. The Silver Skater was a picture of cool nonchalance, as he kickflipped, board-slid and ollied several RAZERs into wide-eyed submission. Hammerhead, meanwhile, employed his shark-senses to sneak up on the robots and take a bite out of their circuit boards, while Nightingale used her very beautiful but very high-pitched singing voice to break the RAZERs' glass eye-panels so that they couldn't see what they were doing, which again resulted in them toppling into the trench.

'I think,' said Peanut, 'that the tide is definitely turning in our favour.'

'Don't speak too soon,' said Jonathan Higginbottom, pointing down and to the right with his tail. 'Look!'

The Big X that had been parked at the end of the North Draw was slowly making its way across into the Green Valleys to help out its fallen comrade.

'The alligator is correct!' said Table Guy. 'And . . . a new danger arrives from the east, also!'

Peanut looked left and saw another Big X, the one previously stationed in Dali Point West, approaching.

'Right,' she shouted. 'Table Guy, how quickly can you get us to the Mission Control room at the top of the Spire?'

'Citizen!' he said, staring into the middle distance as the moonlight painted several highlights on his magnificent quiff. 'Time is but a construct! I am its master, as sure as I am the master of this magnificent solid walnut coffee table, and I vow never to be cowed by the ticking hand, lest it try to enslave me and—'

'Table Guy,' interrupted Peanut. 'That's very poetic and everything, but, seriously, can we get a shift on please?'

'Oh, er, yes!' said the blushing superhero. 'I am sorry, citizen! LET'S FLY!'

54
Green to Red

As they rode their coffee table higher and higher, circling the Spire as they climbed, Peanut pulled Little Tail from her bandolier in readiness.

'Here we are, citizen!' announced Table Guy when they were fifteen metres or so from the very tip at the top. 'Now, go ahead. Be the hero you were born to be and make a difference!'

Peanut drew a large dotted-line oval on the wall, then stepped back.

'OK,' she said. 'Ready? After three: one . . . two . . . THREE!'

The two of them kicked the wall as hard as they could, right in the centre of the oval, and it popped out as if the dotted lines were perforations.

'It worked,' shouted Peanut, before jumping through the hole.

They had judged its position perfectly. She was back in the control room, right next to the missing works of art, opposite the drawings of doors that served as Mr White's personal portals to the real world. She noticed that the one that had the letters 'NYC' stencilled above it was wide open, as was the one with the 'L' above it.

She ran straight over to the console, stood over the buttons, which were all glowing green, and started pressing them as quickly as she could. A few seconds later they were all red.

She ran back to the hole in the wall, and jumped back on to the table.

'Our work here is done,' she said.

'Hey!' replied Table Guy. 'That's my line!'

55

A Victory

Circling the Spire as they descended, Peanut and Table Guy noticed that the Big Xs and the RAZERs had all stopped moving. It had worked! They'd deactivated the robots! Their bird's-eye view of the Resistance forces piling over the drawbridge and into the tower was an amazing sight to behold, and by the time they'd arrived at the bottom of the Spire, it was obvious that the battle was over.

As they touched down amid the deactivated (and cheese-covered) RAZERs and Exocetia, three hovercraft pulled up alongside them.

'PEANUT!' shouted Mr and Mrs M, climbing out of their vehicles.

Peanut jumped from the table and ran over to join the Markmakers in a group hug.

'So much for staying away from the front line,' said Mrs M. 'What *are* we going to do with you?'

Josephine Engelberger climbed out of her vehicle, walked over and held out her hand. 'Peanut Jones,' she said, as they shook. 'It has been a pleasure to serve alongside you and your friends.'

'Speaking of my friends, where are they? Are they OK?'

Suddenly a loud cry came from over near the hole in the crayon fence.

'PEEEEEEEAAAANNUUUTTTTTT!'

Little-Bit came bursting through the crowd of Resistance operatives and leaped into her sister's arms. She was closely followed by Rockwell and Doodle, both looking slightly sheepish in their paint-spattered cheerleader outfits, and Jonathan Higginbottom, whose broad smile lit up the entire island.

'You did it, Peanut,' said Rockwell. 'You've saved the city!'

'*We* did it,' she replied, throwing her arms around him. 'I might have added the finishing touches, but it takes a whole box of paints to make a picture.'

'So, where's Mr White?' said Little-Bit. 'Have we captured him?'

'Our people are searching for him right now,' replied Mrs M. 'We'll find him, don't you worry.'

'I can't believe we've recaptured the Spire,' said Mr M, with tears in his eyes. 'After all these years, we've finally got our city back.'

Peanut, meanwhile, had stepped away from the group and was scanning the crowd intently, looking for the face that she hoped to see more than any other.

'Are you OK, Peanut?' asked Mrs M, moving to stand alongside her.

'Yes, yes. I, er, don't suppose my dad has appeared, has he?' asked Peanut. 'It's just that now we've won the battle, I thought he might not need to stay hidden away any more.'

'Not yet, my girl, not yet,' said Mrs M. 'But I'm sure you'll be reunited very soon.'

'Pardon me for interrupting, citizens!' said a voice from behind them. 'But what do you want us to do with this one?'

They all turned to see Table Guy and Hammerhead flanking a handcuffed and rather cheesy-looking Alan.

'Let's take him to Mission Control,' said Mr M. 'I have one or two questions for him.'

56
The Magic Trick

'et's cut straight to the chase, shall we?' said Mr M, who was sitting in front of the console in Mission Control. 'Where is he?'

Alan lifted his handcuffed hands and brushed away a stringy bit of melted cheese that was dangling from his eyebrow. Then he smiled. 'Where is who?' he said.

'The Easter Bunny,' snapped Peanut. 'Who do you think?'

'Alan,' said Mrs M. 'Tell us where Mr White is hiding.'

'You lot think you're so clever, don't you?' he sneered. 'Now that you've

got your little tower back, you think you rule the world. You think that you've won. Well, let me tell you that you don't and you haven't. And you're not half as smart as you think you are.'

'I can't believe that you, of all people, are saying that,' scoffed Peanut. 'That's like Henry VIII giving out marital advice!'

'Anyway, what are you talking about?' said Rockwell. 'We *have* won! We've got control of the city! We've disabled the RAZERs and the BIG Xs! So *of course* we've won!'

'RAZERs, Big Xs, Exocetia, they're all just toys,' Alan replied, grinning. 'Little toys for little children. The big prize, the *real* prize, is still very much in play.'

'And what prize is that?' said Mr M.

Alan started to laugh. 'You really don't get it, do you? It's all been a magic trick,' he said between giggles.

'What has?' said Mrs M. 'What's been a magic trick?'

Laughing harder now, Alan managed to squeeze out the words 'classic misdirection'.

'OK. I've had enough of this,' said a vexed Mr M. 'WHERE IS MR WHITE?'

Alan was laughing so much, he had tears rolling down his cheeks. Bucket Head, who had accompanied them to the top of the Spire alongside Table Guy, had had enough. He walked over from his position next to the *Mona Lisa*, tipped his head forward and drenched the hysterical man with a few gallons of freezing cold water. It did the trick.

'Now,' said Mr M, once a shivering Alan had composed himself. 'What are you talking about?'

'Do you know what sleight of hand is?' asked Alan.

Mr M shifted slightly in his chair and looked over at his wife. 'Of course I do,' he said. 'It's when someone tricks a person into thinking they're doing one thing when they're actually doing something else altogether. But what's that got to do with anything?'

'When a magician is performing a magic trick in front of you,' said Alan, smiling again, 'he will draw your attention and make you concentrate on this hand –' he held up his left hand – 'while subtly stealing your watch with the other one.'

'What are you telling us?' said Mrs M.

'Well, let's just say that while you've all been concentrating on this little skirmish here in Chroma, you've all had your watches well and truly stolen.'

'Actually, I don't wear a watch,' said Rockwell, smugly.

'So the joke's on you.'

'It was a metaphor,' said Alan, rolling his eyes. 'Good heavens, what *are* they teaching you kids in school these days?'

'OK, that's enough. I think we should lock him up in one of the cells for the night,' said Mr M. 'Give him a taste of his own medicine. I've got a feeling he'll be more willing to talk sense tomorrow.'

As Alan was led away, Peanut suddenly felt nervous.

'Er, Mrs M,' she said. 'I think I'd like to go home, if that's OK. I, er, I just think I really should check on Mum and Leo as soon as possible.'

'I think that's a very good idea,' said the woman. 'But first get some rest – you're exhausted – and then we'll escort you back to the Green Valleys portal first thing in the morning.'

'There's no need for that,' said Peanut, holding up Little Tail. 'Remember?'

57
Homeward Bound

'Once again, the city of Chroma is in your debt,' said Mrs M to the children the next morning as they stood by Peanut's sketch of a door. 'Not only do the citizens have their Spire back, but we've found where Mr White has been storing all of the art equipment that he confiscated over the years. A mountain of creative tools is once again at our disposal! I think it's fair to say that we will be rediscovering our creative mojo over the next days, weeks, months and years as they are redistributed. And that is, in no small part, down to you three.'

Peanut, Little-Bit and Rockwell looked across at the crayon fence. Teams of people were already working hard with their recently reclaimed paints, repairing the hole and returning it to its original, multicoloured glory. Just beyond, they caught a glimpse of the Rainbow Lake, which seemed to be getting lower by the minute. Mr M followed their gaze.

'I know. Not good, is it?' he said. 'Don't worry, we'll work out how White is draining it and do our best to retrieve the missing magical water. At least we know that some of it is in that swimming pool that you found at the top of the Spire. We just need to work out what he's done with the rest.'

'Another reason for us to find him as quickly as possible,' said Mrs M.

'Has Alan still not said anything?' said Rockwell.

'Not yet,' said the woman. 'But he will. We are using a classic persuasion technique. He looks like a man who enjoys his food, so we've put him on a porridge-only diet until he talks. Meanwhile, I have been doing some cooking in the cell next door. The smell of a full English breakfast this morning almost broke him. I'm planning on baking a loaf of bread later, and making a Victoria sponge this afternoon. Trust me, it's only a matter of time.'

'There are some people who want to say goodbye before you go,' said Jonathan Higginbottom. 'I hope that's OK?'

The children looked up at the Spire, just as Table Guy led a procession of saluting superheroes in a fly-past. As the last one (Wonder Walrus) disappeared around the tower and headed back towards Superhero Heights, Mr M clapped his hands, and long, rainbow-striped flags unfurled from every window.

'*Ahhh*,' sighed Peanut. 'It's so good to see colour returning to the city.'

The children said goodbye to a very licky Doodle, then walked over to the door that Peanut had drawn. They waved to the Markmakers and Jonathan Higginbottom as Little-Bit pulled it open.

'I do hope your mum and brother are OK,' said Mrs M.

'Me too,' said Peanut. And with that, they walked through the door.

Part Four

...in which Peanut
Gets Her Wish

I ♥ NY

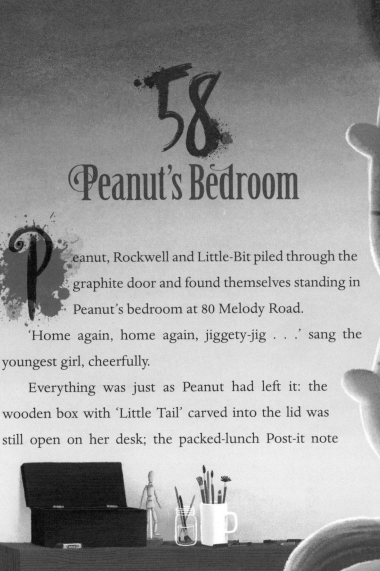

58
Peanut's Bedroom

Peanut, Rockwell and Little-Bit piled through the graphite door and found themselves standing in Peanut's bedroom at 80 Melody Road.

'Home again, home again, jiggety-jig . . .' sang the youngest girl, cheerfully.

Everything was just as Peanut had left it: the wooden box with 'Little Tail' carved into the lid was still open on her desk; the packed-lunch Post-it note

featuring the Hokusai wave was still stuck to her wall; and the drawings that Little-Bit had been looking at were still spread out on the bed.

'It feels like an age since we left,' said Peanut, looking at the clock on her wall, 'But it's only been a few hours.'

'I find that time-difference thing *so* hard to get my head around,' said Rockwell.

Peanut frowned. 'That's odd,' she whispered to herself. 'I don't remember leaving my bedroom door open. In fact, I never leave it op—'

She froze.

So did Rockwell.

A tall boy, with pale skin and red hair, was standing, stock-still, in front of Peanut's bedside table. He was staring straight at them, his mouth open wide, and his eyes even wider.

Little-Bit smiled. 'Hey, Leo,' she said.

The girls' older brother continued to stare at them, unblinking.

'A-a-a door . . .' he stammered. 'The drawing . . . it-it . . . just appeared . . . and . . . and then . . . you came out of it!'

Peanut walked over to him.

'Leo,' she said, gently. 'Where's Mum?'

59
Some Worrying News

'B-b-but . . . you don't understand, Peanut,' said Leo. 'It . . . a door . . . just . . . out of thin air.'

'I know,' she replied. 'There are a lot of things that need explaining, and I promise I will do exactly that.' She swallowed hard. 'But first, tell me, is Mum home or did she go to the ballet?'

'She's not here,' replied the boy. 'She's . . . she's gone away.'

Peanut felt the blood drain from her face.

'Gone away?' she said.

'Y-yes.

'Gone away where?'

'Er . . . I . . . erm . . . Italy. I think. Yes. That's right. Milan.'

'ITALY?' shouted Peanut. 'WHY ON EARTH HAS SHE

GONE TO—?' She suddenly felt a bit dizzy, and everything started to turn white. She sat down on the bed.

Rockwell cleared his throat and stepped forward.

'Hi, Leo. Er, I don't know if you remember me, but I'm Rockwell. We met at the National Portrait Gallery. I'm Peanut's friend.' He put his hand on Peanut's shoulder, which made her feel slightly better. 'I think what she's wondering is, erm . . . who has she gone to Italy with?'

Leo looked at Rockwell. Then he looked at the drawing of the door. Then back at Rockwell. Abruptly, he walked over to the sketch and grabbed the handle. As soon as he touched it, it started to crumble. A few seconds later, it had turned into a pile of silvery grey powder on the floor. 'I think I need to sit down too,' he said.

● ● ●

Five minutes later, Rockwell walked back into the room with a tray holding four steaming mugs of sweet tea.

'Right then, are we feeling any better?' he said.

'A bit,' said Peanut, taking her tea. 'Thank you.'

'Yes. Er, thanks,' said Leo.

'No probs,' said Rockwell. 'OK, Leo, why don't you tell us what happened.'

'Well,' began the boy, 'I left the National Portrait Gallery just after I saw you guys, and came straight back here. When I got home, Mum was in a right state. She was running around, grabbing clothes left, right and centre, chucking them into that little overnight suitcase, and asking me if I'd seen her passport. So, naturally, I asked her what was going on.'

'And what *was* going on?' asked Peanut. 'I thought she was just going to the ballet.'

'She was, er . . . She is. But she said that there had been a last-minute change of plan.'

'A change of plan?'

'Yes. Apparently, just after you and LB had left, her assistant from work turned up at the front door and presented her with two tickets.'

'Yes, that's right. Nerys was just arriving as we left.'

'Well, one of the tickets was for a flight to Milan, and the other one was for a performance of *Swan Lake* at La Scala tomorrow night.'

'What's La Scala?' said Little-Bit.

'One of the most famous ballet theatres in the world, apparently. She said that Mr Stone had managed to get his hands on some tickets at the last minute, and that they must have cost a fortune. He got one for Nerys too, apparently. So she was going to chaperone them, which Mum seemed happy about.'

Peanut started to feel dizzy again. She had a fortifying sip of her tea.

'Did you not think it was a bit weird? Her suddenly heading off to Italy with her boss and her PA?'

'Well, yes. I did say that it seemed a bit extreme to go all that way to watch a bit of dancing. But she insisted that she wanted to go, and she seemed really excited. She said that you two were away on a sleepover anyway, and that she'd ask Leighann to come and babysit tomorrow, when you were back. She said she'd see us on Monday.'

'Peanut, I think we need to stop her getting on that plane,' said Rockwell.

'Too late,' said Leo. 'It took off half an hour ago.'

'Oh no,' said Peanut, standing up. 'I've got a terrible feeling that this was Mr White's plan all along. This must be what Alan was talking about.'

'What do you mean?' said Rockwell.

'All that stuff about magic tricks and sleight of hand. While we were in Chroma concentrating on winning the battle for the Spire, Mr White was back here persuading Mum to go with him to Italy.'

'*The magician will draw your attention and make you concentrate on one hand, while subtly stealing your watch with the other one*,' said Little-Bit, reminding them what Mr White's henchman had said. 'So Mum is the watch?'

'I think she might be,' said Peanut. 'I don't know what to think! At first, I just thought he wanted to steal her from Dad. But now he knows we've got the pencil, and he'll do *anything* to get it back. Maybe he's going to hold her hostage and use her as leverage? He knows we'd do anything to make sure she doesn't come to any harm. What are we going to do?'

'Er, sorry to interrupt,' said Leo, 'but would someone mind telling me (a) who Alan is, (b) what the Spire is, (c) who Mr White is, and (d) why you are describing my mother as a watch?'

Peanut looked over at her brother. It suddenly dawned on her just how much she needed to tell him. She made a mental note to do it as soon as she could, but right now there were more important things to think about.

'As I said, I promise I'll tell you everything,' she said. 'But first, we need to rescue Mum.'

And that's when she noticed it again.

60
The Big Reveal

Leo was holding something small and yellow in his hand.

'What's that?' asked Peanut. 'I noticed it in your pocket at the National Portrait Gallery too.'

He looked at her, a worried expression suddenly appearing on his face. She noticed his eyes kept darting down to her bandolier.

'It's OK. You can tell me,' she said.

He lifted his hand to show her a Post-it note with a bold, geometric shape drawn on it, just like the others stuck to the wardrobe door.

Peanut gasped.

'So it was *you*?' said Little-Bit.

Leo paused, and then nodded slowly.

'Wait,' said Rockwell. 'You're the one who has been putting the Post-it notes in her lunchbox every day?'

'Yes,' replied the boy. He exhaled and looked at his sister. 'And that's not all. You're not the only one with a few things to explain.'

He stood up and walked to the window.

'Peanut, Little-Bit,' he continued. 'I have something I need to tell you both. A secret that I've been keeping for a long time.' But before I tell you, you have to promise that you won't be cross with me for not saying something sooner. I hope you'll see that I didn't have a choice.'

The girls spoke in unison. 'We promise.'

'OK,' he said. 'I think you'd better sit down.'

Leo's Story

know about Chroma,' said Leo, matter-of-factly.
'That is to say, I know that a place called Chroma
exists somewhere, and that it's the hub of all of
the world's creativity.'

'YOU KNOW ABOUT THE ILLUSTRATED CITY?'
shouted an astonished Peanut. 'But . . . but how?'

Leo closed his eyes. 'Dad told me.'

'Dad? But he disappeared over a year ago!'

'Yes. He, er, told me a few months before he . . . went.'

Peanut stared at her brother. She opened her mouth to
speak, but no words came out.

'So, what happened?' asked Little-Bit.

'It was a Sunday afternoon, and you two had gone

somewhere with Mum, probably to Auntie Jean's. Dad called me into his studio and said that there was something important that he needed to tell me, something that Gran had told him when he was eighteen, and that he was going to tell me when I was eighteen. He said that because I was his first-born child, it was my birthright to know.'

'But you weren't eighteen then. In fact, you're *still* not eighteen!' said Peanut, finding her voice again.

'That was my response, too. But Dad said he was telling me early because –' Leo made quote signs with his fingers – '*certain forces* were at play, and he couldn't wait any longer. I got the impression that he was scared of something. That he knew he was in danger. It seemed as though he were telling me as quickly as he could just in case something happened to him.'

'Well, he was right, wasn't he?' said Rockwell.

Leo nodded. 'I guess so.'

'So, what was it he had to tell you?' asked Peanut.

'He said that there was this really important secret city called Chroma, that hardly anyone knew about. He said it was this place in a different dimension where all of the world's creativity sprang from, and that only a few people ever get to visit it. Only those who need it, find it, he said. He said that for generations, knowledge of the city had been passed down through our family, and that it was time that I learned about it. He said he would take me there.'

'So Dad *is* Conté's heir . . .' said Little-Bit, a hushed awe in her voice.

'He is *what*?' said Leo, confused.

'Don't worry, we'll get to that another time,' said Peanut. 'Carry on.'

'OK. Er, where was I? Oh yes. Then a few days later he came into my room and said there was something else he had to tell me about.' Again, Leo glanced down at Peanut's bandolier. 'He mentioned a pencil.'

Peanut's hand automatically went to Little Tail.

'*That* pencil, by the looks of it,' said Leo. 'Dad described it to me: yellow with a handmade feel, a blue eraser and a really long, sharp lead. He said it was the most beautiful pencil you could ever hope to see. Apparently, it's *extremely* important. He also said it was hidden somewhere safe.' He cast a quizzical look at Peanut. 'So, er, where did you find it?'

Peanut picked up the box and showed Leo where the secret compartment was.

'Ah,' said her brother, nodding. 'Makes sense.'

'So, then what happened?' said Little-Bit.

'Dad made me promise not to tell anyone about Chroma or the pencil. Not even Mum. He said the fewer people who knew about it, the safer we would all be.'

'Safer from what?' asked Rockwell.

'He didn't say. But there was definitely something that he was afraid of. He even told me what I should do if he were to ever mysteriously disappear.'

'He did WHAT?' shouted Peanut. 'HE GAVE YOU SOME INSTRUCTIONS?'

'Peanut, you promised you wouldn't get cross with me.'

'BUT . . . BUT YOU KNEW! THE WHOLE TIME! WHAT ABOUT ALL THE FIGHTS I HAD WITH MUM AFTER HE DISAPPEARED?' she screamed. 'WHEN I WAS SAYING HE WOULD NEVER JUST UP AND LEAVE US? THAT HE WOULD NEVER VOLUNTARILY DO THAT TO US? YOU COULD HAVE BACKED ME UP! BUT YOU SAID NOTHING?'

'I had no choice, Peanut! Dad said that if I was to let on that I knew anything, I would be putting you and Mum and LB in terrible danger. He made me swear to keep quiet and not say a word. Don't you think I wanted to tell you everything? Don't you think I wanted to back you up? To make you feel better? I was totally torn! It was awful! The worst time of my life.'

Peanut looked at her brother. He was telling the truth, she could see it in his eyes. She took a breath. She remembered how Leo had changed after Dad had left. He wasn't the same fun-loving, wise-cracking big brother that she had loved so much. He had changed overnight. All of a sudden, he'd spent all of his time either in his room or out 'with friends'. He stopped smiling entirely, instead wearing a permanently anxious expression on his face. Peanut's eyes filled with tears. It all made sense now. She balled her fists and took another deep breath.

'OK,' she said in a much calmer voice. 'I'm sorry, Leo. I understand. I'm not cross any more. It must have been really hard for you.'

'Thanks, Topknot,' he said. 'It was. Actually, I could really use a hug.'

Peanut smiled. It had been a long time since he'd called her Topknot. She put her arms around his waist. It felt really nice to have her big brother back.

'This is all very touching,' said Rockwell, 'but I for one want to hear the rest of the story. Leo, what instructions did your dad leave you?'

'Well, it *was* a bit odd,' replied the boy. 'So odd, in fact, that I had to write them down to make sure I hadn't dreamed the whole thing.'

He stood up and pulled a dog-eared piece of paper from his back pocket and showed it to them.

Go to the National Portrait Gallery and find a security guard called Stanley. He'll be able to help you.

62
The Conduit

O h yes! Stanley!' squawked Rockwell. 'The bloke we saw at the gallery earlier? The one with the little white beard that Mrs M told us all ab—'

'Go on, Leo,' interrupted Peanut.

'He's an amazing man,' continued her brother. 'As brave as a lion, and so supportive. He really helped me when I had no one else to turn to.'

'So, when you first went to the gallery and found him, what happened?' asked Peanut.

'Well, first, he asked me a few questions, just to check that I was who I said I was. As soon as I mentioned Dad's name and the word "Chroma", he trusted me.'

'So did he know where Dad was?'

'Kind of,' said Leo. 'He knew he'd been captured. He had a contact who had seen some intel that said Dad had been taken prisoner by, weirdly, the Mayor of Chroma!'

'Mr White,' said Peanut. 'He's the man who has taken Mum hostage.'

'Hang on, hasn't she gone to Italy with Mr Stone?' said Leo, confused.

'Yes,' said Peanut. 'Oh, it's very complicated, but basically we think Mr Stone and Mr White are the same person.'

'The same person?' said Leo. 'So you're telling me that Mum's boss, that short fella with the oily hair, is also the mayor of a city which only exists in a different dimension? And that he's been keeping Dad prisoner?'

'Yes.'

'Right. Fair enough.'

'Listen, I'll explain everything later, I promise. Finish telling us what happened with Stanley first.'

'I am having the *weirdest* day,' said Leo. 'OK. Where was I? Ah yes, so when Stanley told me that Dad was in prison, that's when we put the emergency plan into operation.'

'The emergency plan?'

'Yes. Apparently, Dad and Stanley were members of some sort of freedom-fighting group in Chroma.'

'The Resistance,' said Rockwell.

'That's the one. And Dad and Stanley had this thing

where if one of them was captured, they'd set up a secret line of communication so that news of their whereabouts or their well-being could be passed on to their loved ones. You just need to establish a conduit.'

'What do you mean a *conduit*?' said Rockwell.

'Something, or someone, that passes information from one place or person to another. Secretly, in this case.'

'So Stanley became the conduit?' said Peanut.

'Exactly,' said Leo. 'He was the link between what was happening in Chroma and what was happening here.'

'What did he tell you?'

'Nothing. Not for a long time, anyway. I had to go to the gallery once a week, check in with him and see if there was any news. This went on for a whole year, and he didn't once have anything to tell me. As far as we knew, Dad was just sitting in a cell somewhere. And then, about three months ago, it changed.'

'Three months ago. That was just after our first trip to Chroma,' said Rockwell to Peanut. This threw Leo slightly.

'Wait, you've *been* to Chroma?' he said, shocked. 'Hang on. Is that what that weird door thing was all about?'

'Yes. But again, I'll fill you in later,' said Peanut. 'Carry on.'

'Er, as I was saying,' said Leo, 'about three months ago it changed. Stanley had something for me.'

'What was it?'

'A Post-it note. With a strange drawing on it. A thick, black L-shape. It also had a little handwritten message saying "Love you forever", followed by a kiss. And it was in Dad's handwriting! I couldn't believe it!'

Rockwell walked over to Peanut's wardrobe, found the note, peeled it from the door and held it up to show Leo.

'You mean this?'

63
A Puzzle

'So Stanley gave you the Post-it note?' said Little-Bit. 'But where did Stanley get it from?'

'OK. Strap in, because this is where it gets even stranger,' said Leo. 'Apparently, a rat turned up in the gallery. Stanley said it appeared from behind a bust of Queen Victoria, and it was holding the note in its mouth.'

'A RAT?' shrieked Rockwell, flinging the note into the air as if it were suddenly on fire. 'I'm scared of rats! Filthy creatures!'

'You're scared of everything,' said Little-Bit dismissively, before turning back to her brother. 'So why did you then hide the note in Peanut's lunchbox?'

'Because, according to Stanley, that's what the rat said I had to do.'

'Whoa!' said Rockwell. 'Rewind! This rat can *talk* now?'

'I told you it got strange,' said Leo.

'So, the *rat* told *Stanley* to tell *you* to hide the note in *Peanut's* lunchbox,' said Little-Bit. 'Why not just give it straight to her?'

'Cos of the whole placing-everyone-in-mortal-danger thing, I guess,' replied Leo. 'It had to remain a secret. Apparently, the rat said that, eventually, Peanut would know what do with the notes.'

'So, at this point, you knew there was going to be more of them arriving?' asked Peanut.

'Yes,' said Leo. 'Stanley said that I needed to come back every day to fetch a new one. In fact, some days there were two, or even three. So that's what I did. Every day, after school, I'd get on the tube and go the National Portrait Gallery. And every morning I'd get up early and hide the new Post-it note between your sandwich and your cereal bar. Thank goodness Mum makes your lunch the night before!'

Peanut picked up the note that Rockwell had thrown across the room and walked over to her wardrobe door. She stuck it back up with the others.

'But . . . Dad was wrong. I *don't* know what to do,' she said. 'What on earth does it all mean? What am I not seeing? Dad, what are you trying to tell me?'

Little-Bit got up and stood next to her sister. She folded her arms and stared at the notes. '*Hmmm*. I wonder . . .' she said.

'Here we go . . .' said Rockwell.

Little-Bit started to move the notes around on the door. She spent about five minutes peeling them off and sticking them back on in different locations, occasionally punctuating proceedings with a 'No, that's not right,' or a 'YES! It fits!' Gradually, her pace picked up until her arms were a frantic blur of activity.

A few minutes later, she stepped away from the door. 'There,' she said triumphantly. 'I've finished.'

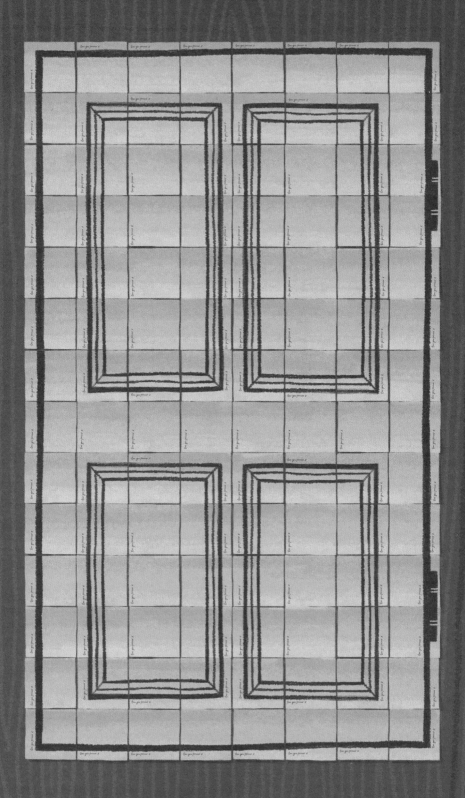

64
Peanut Through the Post-It Notes

Peanut smiled. 'I've said it before, and I'll say it again. Little-Bit, you're a genius.'

'That was astonishing,' said Leo.

'Yeah. I have to admit that was pretty incredible,' said Rockwell, reluctantly. 'Well done, LB.'

'All in a day's puzzling,' replied the little girl. 'Peanut, maybe *this* is the bit where you'll know what to do.'

Peanut looked at her sister. Then she looked at the Post-it note collage and smiled. She pulled Little Tail from her bandolier and got to work.

'Finished,' she said a couple of minutes later.

'I'm not sure it'll work the same way as it has done before, cos the picture is split up into little pieces, but I have a feeling this is what Dad wanted me to try.'

'So y-you're going to open it?' said Rockwell.

'Yes,' she replied. 'And if it works, will you three go through with me?'

Leo and Little-Bit nodded.

'If I must,' said Rockwell.

'OK. Here goes . . .'

Taking a deep breath, Peanut held out her hand, reached into the picture, and grabbed the doorknob that she'd just drawn. It felt cold, as if it were made of brass rather than graphite. She rotated it a quarter turn anti-clockwise. Something clicked.

And then, to their great surprise, the door opened . . .

Dad

'Hello, Peanut,' said the man in the dark room.

She exhaled. And then she smiled.

'Hello, Dad.'

'DADDY!' yelled Little-Bit. She ran straight past Peanut and leaped into her father's open arms, tears streaming down her face. 'I've missed you so much!'

'I've missed you too, beanbag,' he said. 'Oh, you've got so big!'

Leo stepped forward, nervously.

'Dad. I, I . . .'

'I know, son, I know,' said Dad before Leo could say any more. He gently lowered Little-Bit to the floor, then grabbed his son and pulled him in for one of his famous bear hugs. 'I'm SO proud of you, Leo. You did it! You got them here! You're all here!'

Then he looked round at Peanut, his eyes shining in the light that was streaming through the grate.

She smiled, shyly.

'And as for you,' he said. 'My little artist. You're quite the hero, I'm told. Come here, Peanut.'

She cuddled him tightly, burying herself deep in his beardy embrace.

'I always believed in you, Dad,' she said, tears pricking her eyes. 'Always.'

'Ahem,' came a voice from near the Post-it note door.

'Oh, yes,' said Peanut, turning around. 'Dad, this is my friend Rockwell Riley.'

'Pleased to meet you, sir,' said Rockwell. 'I've heard so much about you.'

'Likewise, young man. Thank you for being such a good friend to my girls.'

'Oh, no problem. Being their friend is pretty easy, really.' He looked at Little-Bit, and smiled. 'Well, most of the time. Er, can I ask a question, Mr Jones? Where are we? And what happened after you escaped from the Spire?'

'That's two questions,' said Little-Bit.

'Yes, of course,' said Dad. 'I can see see that you guys need some answers. Well, firstly, I can assure you that we're somewhere safe. We're very close to Chroma, that's all you need to know for now. And as for my escape, I actually had quite a bit of help.'

Suddenly, the two glowing red lights in the corner of the room turned bright green, and a tall silver robot emerged from the shadows.

'*Greetings, Jones children,*' they said in a metallic voice. '*Greetings, Jones children's friend.*'

'RAZER!' yelled Rockwell, before diving under the desk at the back of the room and covering his head with his hands.

'Rockwell,' said Dad. 'There's nothing to worry about. This is 67. They're on our side. Without them, I never would have got out.'

'Gary! Don't forget about me!' A gruff voice, with a broad Glaswegian accent, appeared to be coming from somewhere on the floor near Rockwell. The children looked down, just in time to see a large, brown rat saunter out from under the desk.

Rockwell leaped to his feet, jumped on to the chair and started screaming.

'AARGH! IT'S A RAT!' he howled.

'Kids, this is Woodhouse,' said Dad, stifling a laugh. 'His help has been invaluable. Without him, you wouldn't be here in this room with me now.'

'All right, wee ones? It's grand to finally catch up with you all.'

'A pleasure to meet you too, Woodhouse,' said a smiling Little-Bit. 'And you, 67.'

'Dad, I have to ask,' said Peanut. 'Why didn't you come and help us at the Battle for the Spire?'

Dad walked over to the desk.

'I know it's difficult for you to understand,' he said, 'and heaven knows it was very hard for me to stay away, but according to the stories, Conté's heir is the source of the kind of power White can only dream of. That is a huge threat to him.'

'So if you have this power, why not use it to help with the battle?' asked Peanut.

'I wish I could have, but the secret of how the power works has been lost for many years. Until I can uncover the secret,

I have to stay hidden from White. If he had managed to lure me out into the open, and capture me again, the Resistance would have lost its best chance to destroy White's threat to Chroma once and for all. When I was first imprisoned in the Spire, no one knew I was Conté's heir. But now White knows, he will stop at nothing to get rid of me. I won't jeopardise everything that the Resistance is working towards.'

'Working towards?' said Rockwell from his position atop the chair. 'Ah, of course! You won't have heard the news! We won the battle! The Resistance has control of the Spire! We're not *working towards* anything! Because we've already done it!'

'I did hear the news, actually,' replied Dad. 'I've been keeping a close eye on what's been happening from here.' He pointed at a small, primitive-looking computer on the desk. 'You've all done so much for this city already.'

'So . . . what did you mean by *working towards*?' asked Peanut.

Dad stood up. A shadow seemed to pass across his face. 'I'm afraid, children, that Chroma will never be fully liberated until the day that Mr White is captured. Unless he is physically locked inside a cell, he remains a danger to us and to everything we stand for. To the very existence of creativity.' He walked over to the grates and looked outside. 'You're right, Rockwell. The Battle for the Spire *is* won. But I'm afraid the war is *not* over.'

The room was silent for a good thirty seconds before Peanut spoke.

'Dad, there's something else you need to know.'

He turned to look at her, his eyes wide amid the mass of red hair. 'What is it?'

She took a deep breath. 'He's got Mum,' she said quietly. 'He's taken her to Italy.'

'Who has?'

'Mr White. He wasn't in Chroma when the battle was raging. He was back in London. Apparently, persuading Mum to go to Milan with him was more important than retaining control of the city. We think he might be planning to hold her hostage.'

'NO!' shouted Dad, banging his fist on the wall, which made them all jump. 'Not Tracey! She doesn't even know that Chroma exists!'

'I know,' said Peanut.

'This can't be true! It's me he really wants,' said Dad, blinking hard. 'That must be why he's taken Tracey. He knows I'll go after her.'

'But Dad, when he sent those tickets for Mum, he still had this,' said Peanut, pulling the yellow pencil from her bandolier. 'And now we have it.'

Dad's eyes widened. 'Little Tail,' he gasped. 'Yes! You're right, Peanut! He didn't account for the fact that we would have Little Tail!'

Dad strode over to the large metal door at the far end of the room and opened it. 'Come on,' he said to everyone. 'There's no time to lose.'

'Where are we going?' asked Peanut.

'Italy,' said Dad. 'We're going to rescue your mum!'

Epilogue

The theatre, in the heart of Milan, was unbelievably beautiful. The six rows of balconies, arranged in a giant horseshoe around the stalls, gave every single person in the audience, all two thousand of them, a perfect view of the stage.

Tonight, La Scala's world-famous ballet company was dancing *Swan Lake*.

Mr Stone, wearing a black suit, sat in the centre of the front row. He turned to the woman sitting on his left.

'Tracey darling,' he whispered. 'Do you understand what's going on? I'm a bit lost, I'm afraid.'

A dancer was spinning across the stage, perfectly executing a dizzying run of *fouettés*.

'Well,' said Peanut's mum, 'she is the nasty black swan.

And she's pretending to be the white swan, that we saw earlier. You know, the nice one that the prince is in love with. It's confusing because they're played by the same dancer.'

Mr Stone's pale grey eyes glinted. 'Ah, so it's an old-fashioned *good versus evil* story, is it? Right up my street,' he said.

Nerys, sitting in the row behind them, looked up from her knitting.

'That's just one of the themes,' whispered Tracey. 'It's also about how power can destroy a person, and how having control over everything doesn't necessarily make you happy.'

'Yes, well, I'm not sure about that . . .' said Mr Stone.

Nerys's eyes narrowed.

'But mainly,' continued Tracey, 'the story shows us that people are often hurt the most by those that they're closest to.'

Mr Stone smiled, revealing a set of perfectly straight white teeth.

'Never a truer word spoken, Tracey darling. Throughout history, humans have come up with all sorts of ingenious ways to destroy their enemies, but one simple fact remains . . .'

He put on his white fedora, grabbed her hand, and looked her straight in the eye.

'There is no weapon more powerful than love.'

To be continued . . .

Follow Peanut as her adventure concludes in

COMING IN SEPTEMBER 2023

About the author

Rob Biddulph is a bestselling and multi award-winning author/ illustrator whose books include *Blown Away, Odd Dog Out, Kevin* and *Show and Tell*. In March 2020 he started *#DrawWithRob*, a series of draw-along videos designed to help parents whose children were forced to stay home from school due to the coronavirus pandemic. The initiative garnered widespread international media coverage and millions of views across the globe. On 21 May 2020 he broke the Guinness World Record for the largest online art class when 45,611 households tuned in to his live *#DrawWithRob* YouTube class, and in July 2020 he was named as a Point of Light by the Prime Minister. He lives in London with his wife, their three daughters, Ringo the dog and Catface the cat. He is, for his sins, an Arsenal fan.

Glossary

Campbell's Soup Cans — Andy Warhol

Andy Warhol (1928–1987) was born in Pittsburgh, USA, and is famous for producing paintings and prints. Andy Warhol's most popular work, *Campbell's Soup Cans* (1962), is a set of thirty-two canvases, displayed together just as you would find regular tins of soup on the shelves of a supermarket. Each canvas depicts a different flavour, the original being Tomato. It is a form of 'Pop Art', which refers to art based on popular culture – media or products that were seen in everyday life. He worked from his studio, known as The Factory, which everyone in 1960s New York knew as *the* place to be. *Campbell's Soup Cans* can be seen in the Museum of Modern Art (or MoMA), in New York, USA.

Salvador Dali (1904–1989)

Salvador Dali is an important surrealist painter and printmaker born in Figueres, Spain, in 1904. He is perhaps most famous for creating the *Mae West Lips Sofa* with his British patron Edward James, and his painting *The Persistence of Memory* (1931), which is considered one of the masterpieces of the twentieth century.

He is also known for his painting *The Elephants*, which depicts two elephants with long spindly legs on an otherwise barren background.

The Empire State Building

The Empire State Building is a 102-storey skyscraper in Midtown Manhattan, in New York City. Built in the Art Deco style in 1931, it is still one of the world's tallest buildings. It is an American cultural icon, and is well known for featuring in the movie *King Kong*.

Joseph Engelberger (1925—2015)

Josephine Engelberger, designer and inventor of the RAZERs, is inspired by the real life Joseph Engelberger, who was an American engineer born in Brooklyn, New York, in 1925. He is most famous for his contribution to automated production lines and is today considered the 'father of robotics'.

Galileo (1564—1642)

Galileo Galilei, often referred to as just Galileo, was born in Pisa, Italy, in 1564. He was an Italian astronomer, physicist and engineer, and was a great contributor to the development of the telescope. His lenses allowed a magnification greater than any telescope of the time, and through these he was able to see the Moon's craters, Jupiter's moons and the stars of the Milky Way, to name just a few.

The Great Wave Off Kanagawa — Katsushika Hokusai

The Great Wave Off Kanagawa is considered one of the most recognisable pieces of Japanese art. It was created by the Japanese artist, painter and printmaker Katsushika Hokusai, born in Edo (now Tokyo), Japan, in 1760.

Guernica — Pablo Picasso

Guernica is an oil painting on a large canvas, and is one of Pablo Picasso's best-known works. Picasso was inspired by a terrible bombing raid on the town of that name in 1937, and the painting depicts the tragedy of war. It is one of the most powerful anti-war symbols in the world. It can be found in the Museo Reina Sofía, in Madrid, Spain.

The Hay Wain — John Constable

The Hay Wain is an oil-on-canvas painting depicting a rural scene on the River Stour by landscape painter John Constable, who was born in Suffolk, England, in 1776. The River Stour is an East Anglian river between the English counties of Suffolk and Essex. *The Hay Wain* can be found in the National Gallery in London. 'Wain' is another word for 'wagon'.

The Jinou Yonggu Cup

The Jinou Yonggu Cup, which translates into English as the 'Cup of Solid Gold', belonged to the Emperor Qianlong, and was created in 1739 as a birthday present to him. The cup is made of gold, pearls and diamonds, and is one of the greatest treasures of the so-called 'Forbidden City' in Beijing.

The Louvre

The Louvre is a museum of art and archaeology, which first opened its doors in 1793. It is one of the world's most-visited museums, and is a central landmark in France's capital city, Paris. It is home to some of the world's best-known paintings and sculptures, including the *Mona Lisa*, and the *Venus de Milo*.

MoMA

The Museum of Modern Art (MoMA) is an art museum which first opened in 1929. It is one of the world's largest and most famous modern art museums, and is a central landmark in New York City, located as it is in Midtown Manhattan. It is home to a vast collection of modern and contemporary art pieces.

Mona Lisa — Leonardo da Vinci

The *Mona Lisa* (roughly translated to My Lady Lisa) is probably Leonardo da Vinci's best-known work. This little painting has had many admirers, has come under attack, and was even stolen in 1911. Today, The *Mona Lisa* can be seen in the Louvre, in Paris, France.

Isaac Newton (1642–1727)

Isaac Newton was a mathematician, author and astronomer, among other things, who was born in England in 1642. He is best remembered for developing our understanding of modern physics, including the laws of motion and gravity.

Queen Victoria — Sir Joseph Edgar Boehm

The Queen Victoria bust mentioned in the story was made by Sir Joseph Edgar Boehm, a sculptor born in Vienna, in 1834. He moved to London in 1848, and is most famous for creating the coinage portrait of the so-called 'Jubilee head' of Queen Victoria in 1887. He was also known for creating portrait busts, many of which can be seen in the National Portrait Gallery in London.

Bridget Riley (1931–present day)

Rockwell's mother, Bridget Riley, is named after the British painter who was born in Norwood, London, in 1931. The real

Bridget Riley is most famous for her abstract paintings and monochrome artwork – a taste for which Rockwell's mother shares – which puts colours, shapes and patterns together in a way that creates an optical illusion and can look as if it is moving.

Unknown Woman, formerly known as Mary Shelley – Samuel John Stump

The painting *Unknown Woman, formerly known as Mary Shelley* is an oil-on-canvas portrait which may depict the writer Mary Shelley, now most famous for her gothic novel *Frankenstein* (1818). This painting was made by Samuel John Stump, who was a miniature and landscape painter born in England in 1778, and can be seen in the National Portrait Gallery in London.

Venus de Milo – Alexandros of Antioch

Venus de Milo is a marble statue depicting the Greek goddess of love. It was made by the sculptor Alexandros of Antioch, born between 130 and 100 BCE. The sculpture can be found in Paris's Louvre museum.

Acknowledgements

A lot of people assume that writing (and illustrating) a book is a thing that a person does on their own. They think that we sit at our laptops and tap away for a few months, and then, as if by magic, a book suddenly appears on the shelves of bookshops across the world. This couldn't be further from the truth. There are so many people that have worked really hard to help bring Peanut's adventures to the page, and I am now going to attempt to credit as many of these heroes as I can.

First up is Sarah Hughes, my brilliant editor, whose superpowers were invaluable when it came to wrestling my story into shape, and making sure that all of the loose threads were tightened. Time and time again, she lifted the narrative and made it fly. For that I can't thank her enough.

I'd also like to thank Amy Boxshall, Nick de Somogyi and Fraser Crichton for copy-editing and proofreading the manuscript, Laura Carter for production control, Charlie Castelletti for compiling the glossary, Elena Koumi for the sensitivity read, and Melissa Pesce for checking my French. Legends, all of you.

Not only are my design team at Macmillan Children's Books brilliant, but they are also very lovely to work with. Becky Chilcott was my trusted guide as I attempted to scale this particular illustration mountain, providing wise words, a kind hand and great support as I struggled through more than a hundred and seventy drawings. This expedition would have been a failure without you, Becky. Similarly, industry legend Chris Inns somehow managed to cajole a fabulous cover out of me, one that might be my favourite to date. Thanks, as ever, Chris. Massive shout-out too, to Tony Fleetwood, not only for coping with my rather unwieldy photoshop files, but for making such mind-bogglingly brilliant animated trailers for the book.

I'd also like to thank the wider Pan Macmillan team, led by the brilliant Belinda Rasmussen, for making this book an actual, real-life thing, and getting it out there into the world and into the hands of readers. So thank you to Jo Hardacre, Alison Ruane, Alyx Price, Charlie Morris, Sarah Clarke, Rachel Graves, Amber Ivatt, Sarah Plows, Sabina Maharjan and Louisa Sheridan. I love working alongside you guys.

A special thank you to my old friend Iain Church, or, to give him his proper title, Lieutenant Colonel Iain Church, Royal Engineers (Retired), for his invaluable help with the military lingo used during the big battle scene in Chroma. Considering the first draft that I sent you must have been totally baffling (ink bombs, illustrated trebuchets powered by illustrated hamsters, cartoon vikings firing bazookas, etc.) you did a fantastic job of bringing some realism and credibility to it. I am in your debt, sir.

None of this would have happened in the first place were it not for my brilliant agent Jodie Hodges, plus Emily Talbot and Molly Jamieson, her team at United Agents. I've said it before but I'll say it again, I am lucky to have the best people in my corner.

Thanks, also, to the booksellers, librarians, teachers, bloggers and reviewers who continue to support me throughout my career. Your good opinion is so important to me, and I never, ever take it for granted.

Massive thanks to my team of early readers: Greg, Noah and Sam Corke, Alan and Lula Stainton, Sylvia Biddulph (mum), Paul Biddulph (dad), Daniel Biddulph (brother), and Amanda Hudgell (sister). I know I can trust you to be honest, so thank you for being just that. I am glad (and relieved) that you enjoyed the book.

Finally, thank you to my daughters, Ella, Kitty and Poppy for putting up with me working all the time, to my dog Ringo for keeping me company in the studio on those late nights, and to my wife Ally, who is always my first (and my favourite) reader. Truth be told, as long as she likes it, I'm happy.